Secrets

Jade Winters
&
Alexis Bailey

Secrets

by Jade Winters & Alexis Bailey

Published by Wicked Winters Books

WICKEDWINTERS

ISBN: 978-1-508-61555-2

Other titles by Jade Winters

Novels

143
A Walk Into Darkness
Caught By Love
Guilty Hearts
Say Something
Faking It
Second Thoughts

Novellas

Talk Me Down From The Edge

Short Stories

The Makeover
The Love Letter
Love On The Cards
A Story Of You
Neighbour From Heaven

For Ali, as always

Chapter One

I need one more minute. Just one more … Lauren's hand slowly snaked its way from beneath the duck feather quilt and silenced the alarm with a hard smack. Although she knew she was pushing her luck to get to work on time, she wasn't quite ready to face the world yet. *Mondays! Ugh.* Lauren could hear the shower running in the en-suite bathroom, accompanied by an out of tune melody. She'd never understand Calum in a million years. She loved her husband, but, seriously, it just wasn't normal to be so cheerful and singing in the shower on a Monday morning. Or any morning for that matter.

"Good morning, beautiful!" Calum sang out as he exited the bathroom with a towel wrapped around his waist. After two years of married life and knowing that she was no one's bride, but Frankenstein's, Calum still called her beautiful every morning. Lauren glared at him as laughter lines deepened around his mouth. It wasn't personal – she would have glared at Santa Claus if he'd woken her up on Christmas morning. As Calum strode towards the wardrobe and opened the doors, Lauren rolled onto her side and stroked their miniature dachshund, Scruff, who was sound asleep in Calum's space.

"You're the only truthful one around here, aren't you, sweetheart?" she said, scratching his ear.

Scruff cracked open an eye and thumped his tail

at her. She smiled, then reluctantly pushed back the cover and slipped out of bed.

"Please don't talk to me until I've drunk at least a gallon of coffee," she said, briefly skimming her palms across Calum's satin smooth back as she passed him and made her way down to the kitchen.

As she entered the contemporary space, she noted the coffee pot was already half empty, confirming that Calum had been up for a while. BBC News 24 played quietly on the small integrated TV screen above the black granite worktop. Lauren guessed that Calum already knew everything that had happened overnight. He had always been like that – keeping abreast of current events. Well, at least for as long as she had known him, which was almost eight years now. They had first met as sixteen-year-olds at secondary school. Calum had been one of the best debaters on the debate team.

He had been standing at the podium leading a current events discussion when she'd walked into the classroom for her first meeting. He reminded her of Superman – tall and athletic with jet black hair and piercing blue eyes. With his school tie and immaculate striped blazer, he looked so professional and mature as he argued his point with his deep, articulate voice.

Now eight years later, he still looked the same in his white open-necked shirt and black trousers as he walked into the kitchen and gave her a quick peck on the cheek. He had one more year to go on the foundation programme, followed by several more years of vocational training. Eventually Lauren would be married to a fully qualified doctor.

"What time is your assessment today?" she asked as Calum sat down at the table and poured out a bowl of cereal.

"At two o'clock." He spooned a mouthful of food past his lips and chewed absent-mindedly. After a few seconds, he continued, "Then I've got a meeting to discuss my next placement."

Lauren watched as he picked up his mug and drank the last dregs of his coffee. It always amazed her to think that Calum had been her one and only boyfriend *ever*! Although they'd split up several times through secondary school and university, the break ups had never lasted, and Lauren had always remained faithful to him.

Sure, over the years she had certainly fantasized about other men. Well, that wasn't exactly true. She'd fantasized about other … *other women*. There. She'd said it. She couldn't even begin to understand why she had those kinds of fantasies. She wasn't a lesbian. She'd never kissed another woman, let alone been attracted to one in real life. Yet, when Calum made love to her, in her mind's eye there were always strong and vivid images of faceless women. A rush of heat would flood her body as she imagined her tongue skimming over a woman's glistening inner thigh. Of teasing a tight rosy nipple between her fingers or losing herself in the soft velvet warmth of a woman's kiss.

Maybe it was natural to feel this way after sleeping

with the same man for eight years. She was only twenty-four, and her life already revolved around a set routine. She worked Monday to Friday at her parent's antique shop, restoring furniture and invoicing. She chatted with customers about their projects and went to auctions to look for deals for their shop.

In the evenings, she made dinner, folded laundry and either read or watched a documentary on the National Geographical Channel. Calum had worked irregular hours for at least the past two years while finishing up medical school. So, she was usually on her own because even if he was home, he was studying or trying to catch a few hours of sleep. Yes, her life was dull, dull, dull!

"Right, I'm off," Calum said as he stood and put his bowl in the sink. Lauren was leaning against the counter drinking her coffee, whilst half listening to the morning news. Death, more death, terrorism and job losses. *Honestly, if I hear one more piece of negative news, I'm going to scream.*

Calum rounded on her and pressed his body up against hers. It took less than two seconds for Lauren to realise what he had on his mind.

"No way," she said laughing as she pressed her palms against his chest and pushed him away.

Calum took a step back. "Oh, come on, babe," he pleaded with a pout more suited to a two-year-old child. "There's nothing to stop us having a quickie."

"Cal, surely you should know by now I'm not a morning person. I've barely got the energy to get ready for work, let alone have a shag."

A smirk spread across his face. "But what am I going to do about Teddy," he said, pointing towards the obvious bulge in his trousers.

"Take a cold shower or …" She reached up and pinched his cheek. "Think about the time you saw your Aunt Frieda in her birthday suit."

"Oh, yuck." Calum's expression turned into a scowl. "Talk about killing the moment."

"Go on go, off to work now," she said, shooing him away with a flick of her hand.

He laughed as he took a step forward and kissed her forehead. "I love you."

"You too. Good luck and let me know if you'll be home for dinner."

"Um, sure," he responded with a nervous chuckle.

She ran the tip of her finger down his chest. "I'll serve it in bed," she teased. "We can play doctors and nurses afterwards if you like," she added suggestively.

Calum raised his brows, his eyes suddenly hopeful. "In that case, I'll definitely be home for dinner."

Lauren playfully slapped his shoulder. "Oh, so you'll make time in your busy schedule for sex but not for one of my home-cooked meals," she said, feigning insult.

Calum grinned. "Lauren, we both know that cooking is not your strongest attribute. Whereas sex …"

As if in total agreement, Scruff appeared at the kitchen door and let out a bark before walking over to join them. Calum knelt down and scratched behind his ears.

"See, even Scruff agrees with me. Don't you boy?" he said as Scruff rolled over to have his belly rubbed.

Scruff had been living with them for two years now. He was eight pounds of chocolate-coloured cuteness, and they both adored him. He was playful and smart, and without a doubt Lauren's loyal companion, following her around the house wherever she went. Scruff was also a local favourite at the antique shop, and she feared he was going to turn into twice his size soon if people didn't stop bringing him treats.

Lauren snorted. "Well, he would agree with you, being male and all."

Calum stood back up and stretched. Lauren thought he looked tired, but he would never admit it. Calum was so driven and dedicated. She knew he loved her, but sometimes she wondered how he planned to fit her and a family into his life filled with sick and dying people.

"Us men have got to stick together, you know," he said with a playful glint in his eyes.

"I'm sure," she said, grinning. "So, I'll see you tonight then?"

"Mmmmmm." Calum grabbed her around the waist. He kissed her deeply this time. "You have a date. I'm not a fully qualified doctor, yet. But I can definitely play one." He chuckled as he gave her an exaggerated wink. "Gotta run, babe."

"Ok, see you later," she called after him as he grabbed his coat off the back of the chair. Then he was gone.

Lauren picked Scruff up and kissed the top of his head. "I'm afraid I've got to make a move as well," she said as Scruff looked at her expectantly. She normally took him to work with her, but her next door neighbour was looking after him for the day as he had an appointment at the vet's.

An hour later, and a good thirty minutes late leaving for work, Lauren left for the tube station. Her life *really* was like Groundhog Day: it was the same routine over and over again. What did she expect? Nothing out of the ordinary ever happened in her life, so why would today be any different?

Chapter Two

Lauren and Calum lived ten minutes from Highgate tube station, which made commuting to work very easy for them. Parking in London was becoming more and more of a nightmare, with congestion charges and lack of spaces, not to mention traffic jams. Just being the two of them, they were fine using trains and cabs. Now and then, if they took off for a romantic weekend in the country, they just rented a car.

Half way down the escalator, Lauren heard the train screeching to a halt on the tracks. *Oh shit!* She could be late but missing this train was going to be pushing it, even for her. She ran down towards the platform, managed to jump through the train doors just as they closed and banged into the side of someone holding onto the rail.

"I am so sorry!" she exclaimed after hearing a "Whoa!" somewhere in the collision. Righting herself as the train began to move, she looked up past the arm she had collided with and into the verdant eyes of the most attractive woman she had ever seen. *Oh my God!*

The woman laughed, then asked, "Are you okay?" as she flicked back her thick ink-black tresses that danced loosely around her shoulders

Wow. She's talking to me. Say something! "Er … Yes, sorry," Lauren said, trying to compose herself. *Stop acting like a complete idiot.* "I'm running a little behind this morning and thought I was going to miss the train," she rambled on.

"No worries at all." The woman smiled at her. "Been there more times than I care to remember."

"I hope I didn't hurt you," Lauren said, giving her the once over, searching for a flaw. *Surely no woman can be this perfect!* She eyed her from her sculptured facial features right down to her slim, shapely legs encased in a pair of dark blue designer jeans and knee length boots. Perfect!

"I'll survive," she said, revealing a white smile.

"Um, good and er … thanks for serving as a barrier," Lauren said sheepishly as she lowered her gaze to the ground. She thought she'd faint if she looked into her eyes again.

"Anytime."

Lauren turned reluctantly, then walked along the carriage to the next available seat and planted herself down. Now she could relax. She had a twenty minute ride to King's Cross where she would change to the Piccadilly line for another twenty minute journey, and then a ten-minute walk to work. She pulled her phone out of her jacket and flipped through the photos of Calum and Scruff. She needed something to dislodge the memory of the dreamboat she'd just bumped into. Moments later her eyes involuntarily glanced up again. The woman had left her spot holding onto the rail and had settled in a seat four rows up from where she sat. From her vantage point, Lauren could look at her without the woman noticing. She had taken out, what looked like, an academic book. One long leg was crossed over the other, and she appeared to be quite engaged in what she was reading.

Lauren settled back in her seat, resting her head against the cold glass window. She closed her eyes and slowly a vision began to unfold behind her eyelids.

The lights in the bar are low, giving the room an intimate feel. The woman from the train is sitting alone, drinking champagne from a long stemmed glass. She's wearing an off-the-shoulder top, revealing smooth, lightly tanned skin. I take a seat next to her, my senses swimming from the scent of the heady perfume she wears. She turns and looks at me as she slides her bottom lip between her teeth. I can feel my temperature rising as she lowers her thick, black lashes and asks me if I want to share her drink.

I nod my head slowly. I feel as if I'm falling under a hypnotic spell. As I take the glass of champagne, our fingertips touch and a strange tingling sensation grips my body like a vice. Her green eyes study me intently, as I take a small sip of the pale-coloured liquid. I wince sharply as the bitter tasting bubbles dance on my tongue. Suddenly the woman leans against me and her touch awakens every nerve in my body. The atmosphere is so intoxicating, even the air seems to be holding its breath.

"Do you want to have a drink somewhere more private? I've got a room here," she asks in a quiet whisper as she strokes the inside of my thigh with the tip of her finger.

I'm lost in the woman's eyes. I'd agree to anything if it meant being alone with her. Again I nod and the woman slips from her seat and heads for the exit. Full of anticipatory adrenaline, I follow her to the lift. The way she walks carries its own kind of excitement. We travel up to the hotel room on the fifth floor in silence, our eyes alive with the anticipation of what we both know is coming.

"Take a seat," the woman instructs me in a velvet edged voice, before disappearing into the bathroom.

I cross the room and take a seat on a plush chair by the window. My hands are trembling and my breathing speeds up as my heart pounds against my rib cage. I know it's too late to back out now, but I wouldn't even if I could. This is what I want. What my body needs! To be fucked by this gorgeous, hot woman. Why should I deny myself such pleasure?

The bathroom door opens and the woman steps out. I am enraptured by her but at the same time, filled with a strange fear. My eyes are riveted on her nakedness. Tall, slender and graceful – a lethal combination. Fascinated, I watch as she walks towards me and stops a few feet in front of me. She drops to her knees and crawls across the carpeted floor until she reaches my open thighs.

I dare to meet her exacting gaze. She reaches up, and her finger slowly trails along my jaw line before moving defiantly to my mouth and slipping in between my lips. I can tell by the challenging gleam in her eyes that she is enjoying the effect she is having on me. I am a lioness being tamed by an expert tamer. Her finger caresses my tongue before coming to an abrupt halt. I widen my eyes in surprise. I want to feel her inside me, but I say nothing, because she's in control. The very thought of being submissive to this woman makes my clit ache with such need that it takes every ounce of willpower I have not to reach down between my legs and caress myself right there and then.

Without saying a word she begins to undress me,

tantalisingly slow, brushing her fingers over my erect nipples as she unbuttons my shirt. Next she removes my jeans, pulling them off in one swift movement. The back of her hand rubs firmly against my clitoris before she removes my underwear. Suddenly I'm naked and exposed but I don't feel vulnerable – I feel horny and ready for anything and everything she wants to do to me. My juices are leaking down my thighs onto the seat beneath me. I wiggle a little as she ducks her head down between my legs – I can feel the heat of her tongue as she blazes a trail towards my throbbing centre. Time has stopped. I have forgotten everything, even what I am doing here. My body quivers with a desire I've never felt before. I move my hands down to her head, tugging a handful of hair when her tongue makes contact with my pulsating clit. Minutes later, I'm suddenly hit with a sensation that ripples through my body, causing me to arch my back as waves of ecstasy flood through me. She lifts her face to meet mine, a vixen smile on her swollen lips. I lean forward, anticipating her mouth on mine, desperate to taste her for the first time. Just as I feel her lips....

"King's Cross Station!" The loud announcement jolted Lauren out of her fantasy. Coming to her senses, she scrambled to her feet and ran for the closing doors. Too late – the train started moving again. *What the … ?!!! Oh my God!!! Seriously?* Lauren frantically looked around. *Well, that's just great! Arrgghhh.* She had missed her stop. How could she have done that?

Lauren let out a heavy sigh and sat back down. She looked up at the row of seats; the woman was nowhere to be seen. A ghost of a smile flickered across Lauren's mouth. *Now she was definitely worth being late for!*

Chapter Three

Lauren finally arrived at work. She was only an hour late, but her mother scowled at her as if she'd missed the whole week. The antique shop consisted of two large rooms. There was the showroom which had the floor displays, some "before and after" examples, and also some pieces for sale. The adjoining room, that was partitioned off by a half wall, was the back workroom. There was a desk and filing cabinet for the paperwork, and a table and chairs for eating lunch. The rest of the space was taken up with various projects and the tools, machines, work tables and other equipment needed to keep "Tate's Antique Restoration and Repair" up and running. To the right of the back workroom was another area where her and her parents' offices were located.

"Busy morning?" her mum, Jean, asked sarcastically as soon as she caught sight of Lauren rushing towards her office. Though she was a dainty woman, with delicate hands and fair features, she was a formidable force to deal with if you got on the wrong side of her.

"You have no idea," Lauren said. She wasn't comfortable just outright lying to her mother, but she was ok with keeping it generic. What was she supposed to say? *Well, what happened was, I almost missed the train. But I didn't. I made it by bumping into the most gorgeous woman on the planet. I then spent the next twenty minutes fantasizing about all the things I wanted her to do to me, which made me miss my stop.*

Lauren laughed at the very thought of being so honest; her mother would surely collapse from the shock of it.

"What's so funny?" Jean asked, taking Lauren by the arm and leading her towards her own office a couple of doors down.

"Nothing. I was just thinking about something Calum said this morning."

As they entered the office, Jean shut the door behind them and leaned against it, letting out an exaggerated breath. "I need to talk to you about–"

"–Look, if this is about me being late again …"

Jean brushed away an imaginary speck of dirt from the lapel of the salmon-coloured jacket she wore. "This is nothing to do with that. I need to talk to you about a more delicate issue."

Lauren frowned. "Is Nan okay?"

Lauren loved her grandmother dearly, and it seemed like every time she saw her lately, the poor woman seemed frailer.

Jean nodded her head. "Yes, your Nan's still the same. Look, take a seat," she said, making her way around her antique desk and lowering herself onto the upholstered chair.

Lauren slid into the seat opposite. She knew better than to flop onto the expensive chair. The last time she haphazardly dropped into one of them, she had gone straight through it – to say her mother was not the slightest bit amused would be an understatement.

Lauren briefly glanced towards the antique clock on the wall. "So what's up?"

"It's … well … there's …"

She raised her eyebrows. "Come on, Mum, spit it out. Whatever it is can't be that bad."

Jean leaned forward and toyed with a pen on her desk. "Money's going missing from the company accounts."

Lauren's curiosity was piqued. Her mother had her full attention now. "What do you mean going missing? How? Who?"

"The accountant has done our end of year accounts and says there are discrepancies." She dropped the pen from her hand and leaned back in her chair. "I don't know who's responsible. But that's not to say I don't have my suspicions."

"What does Dad have to say about it all?"

Jean lowered her eyes, avoiding Lauren's incredulous stare.

Fury almost choked Lauren as her eyes widened. "Mum, please tell me you've told him."

"Not exactly, no," Jean said sheepishly.

Lauren leapt from her seat and took an abrupt step forward. "Oh, be fair, will you. He has a right to know. This is the problem; you treat Dad as if he's one of your employees, not an equal partner."

Jean's mouth tightened in response to the challenge in Lauren's voice. "You don't know what you're talking about Lauren. I've been more than fair to your father all these years considering …"

Lauren narrowed her eyes. "Considering what? Considering the company belongs to your family, and he has no say in the running of things?"

"You've always sided with your father, haven't you?" Jean said, with a small shake of her head.

Lauren ignored her comment and walked towards the door. She couldn't support her mother's treatment of her father. She had noticed that things between them had been getting worse over the past few months. Whatever the problem was, neither of them ever spoke about it. Their unresolved issues remained the elephant in the room.

"Is that it then, nothing more to say on the matter?" Jean asked in a far harsher tone than Lauren had ever heard her use before.

Lauren threw her hands up in the air. "I'm not getting involved in your fights. If you don't want to tell him, that's up to you. But you're just putting another nail in the coffin. If he ever finds out you lied to him–"

Jean interrupted her vehemently, "–Lauren, I'm sorry to have to disappoint you but this time it isn't me that's in the wrong."

Lauren gave a half-hearted shrug. "Yeah okay, whatever you say." She opened the door and took a step out into the corridor. Before she had time to close it behind her, she heard her mother's voice quiver and break before becoming stronger. "Lauren, your father's the one who's responsible for the missing money."

Chapter Four

Did I just hear right? Lauren was temporarily speechless. She spun around and stared at her mother who was still seated in her chair. Her steely blue eyes looking up at her dejected.

Lauren didn't know how to respond. She walked tentatively into the office and gently closed the door behind her. "Mum, do you know what you're saying?" she asked as she neared the desk.

Jean nodded. When her eyes met Lauren's they were moist with tears.

"Why would he need to steal money from the company? You're both well off."

"It's complicated, Lauren."

Lauren gave a bitter laugh. "Oh, no you don't. Don't start all this cloak and dagger secrecy. I'm sick of being piggy in the middle between you two."

"Calm down and take a seat." Jean sighed with exaggerated patience.

Lauren did as she was told. "Right, I'm calm and I'm ready to listen."

Jeans fingers twisted her gold wedding band. "Okay, you asked for it. You want to know the truth about your father, I'll tell you. For the past five months, I've suspected that he has been having an affair."

Lauren stifled a laugh. "Dad? Yeah right!"

"That's what I thought at first. But I can't turn a

blind eye to it any longer. Not now that it's going to put people's jobs at risk."

Lauren's eyes blinked in bewilderment. "I don't understand. What have your suspicions got to do with Dad stealing money?"

"Well, he has to pay for his floozy somehow, doesn't he?" Her voice shook with anger.

Lauren had a hard time getting her head around this bombshell. *A mistress and a secret stash of money?* This sounded nothing like the father she knew. "Have you got any proof to back this up?"

Jean squirmed under Lauren's stare. "Not as yet but I will have shortly."

A surge of defiance swelled inside her. "Well, until then, I won't believe a word of it. And I suggest you do the same."

Lauren made a hasty retreat and headed back to her office. *What utter nonsense.* Her mind still spinning, she hung her jacket on the back of her chair and checked the phone messages her mother had left on her desk. Flipping through them, she saw that they were mostly clients wanting estimates on various pieces they had or were checking the status of current projects Tate's was working on for them.

She couldn't even bear to think of her dad being dishonest in any way. If it turned out to be true, she wouldn't be able to trust another living soul. If her dad could be a wolf in sheep's clothing that meant anyone could be, even Calum.

A sense of guilt crept over her. Was thinking

about having sex with a woman being deceitful? She wondered how Calum would feel if he somehow found out that she was lusting after women. Not very happy she suspected. She pushed the thoughts aside. Just thinking of the implications of her "innocent fantasies" made her shudder.

She heard the front door chime, signalling a customer had entered the shop.

"I've got it, Lauren," her mother called out as she passed Lauren's office.

"Good," she muttered to herself. She wasn't in the mood to deal with anyone today. At least not until she had time to speak to her dad about her mother's accusations. She poured herself a cup of coffee from the brewer she kept in her office. Sitting at her desk with the cup between her hands, her mind was buzzing with different scenarios of how the money could have disappeared. A light-fingered staff member? An incompetent accountant? Her mother blowing things out of proportion, as usual?

"Hey, sweetheart," her dad, Ken, peeked his head in through her office door. At fifty, he was still a good looking man who kept himself fit and trim by going to the gym several times a week. His glossy jet black hair had yet to see one strand of grey.

"Hi, Dad. How's it going?" She twisted awkwardly in her seat. For the first time in her entire life, she felt uncomfortable in her father's presence. She didn't know what to say to him or even if she should broach the subject of him siphoning company funds for his mistress.

Should she say, *"Hey Dad, Mum said you're a two-timing bastard, and you've been stealing company money to keep your floozy in the lifestyle she's become accustomed to. Is she right?"* No, she didn't think that would go down too well somehow.

His voice broke into her thoughts. "Oh, as well as can be expected. How about you?"

Lauren's dad was always upbeat and easy-going. Her mother, on the other hand, tended to be the worrier of the two, not to mention highly suspicious of people. Maybe that was why she had cast suspicion so quickly on her dad. She couldn't think of any other reason why she'd suspect him so resolutely. Surely her dad should have been the last person to accuse rather than the first.

Before she could respond, her phone started to ring. She looked down at it, then towards her dad.

"Answer it, Lauren. I'll catch up with you later." Then his head disappeared from view.

Relieved the moment of truth had been narrowly averted, Lauren picked up the phone and spoke for several minutes with the caller. She had just hung up the phone to Mrs. Springer who was calling to make sure her "priceless Victorian chest" would be ready for delivery on Thursday, when her mum came in and sat down in front of Lauren's desk.

"So I take it you've spilt the beans to your father?"

Lauren sighed. "As a matter of fact I haven't said a word."

Jean wrung her hands together. "Good. I'd like it to stay that way until this mess has been cleared up."

"So you want me to lie to him," Lauren asked, cocking her head to one side.

"No, Lauren, not lie," she said sharply. "Just don't say anything. If he asks, tell him the truth if you want. I'm just asking you not to mention it unless need be."

Lauren felt reassured that she wasn't necessarily bound by secrecy. "So how are you planning to sort out this *mess* as you call it?"

Jean stood, her tone thawing as she spoke. "Come with me to my appointment in half an hour and find out."

Lauren frowned. "Um … where?"

"To see Ms. Andrews?"

Lauren stared at her mother, desperate to understand what in the world she was talking about.

"Gillian Andrews, the forensic accountant I hired to get to the bottom of all this. If anyone can find out where all the money has gone, it will be her."

"A forensic accountant!" exclaimed Lauren. "You're really serious, aren't you? You think Dad's responsible. Come on, Mum. Can't we sort this out between us?"

Jean dismissed her question with a wave of her hand. "No, we can't, Lauren. How will things look if I don't investigate this? What sort of message will we be giving our employees? That there's one rule for us and one rule for them. No, a thief is a thief in my book," she said with finality.

Lauren's shoulders slumped. "So what are you going to do if it turns out you're right about Dad?"

"I'll file for divorce. If there's no trust in a relationship, then there's nothing else as far as I'm concerned."

Lauren rolled her eyes. "Bloody great. I'm going to be the product of a broken home."

"Don't be silly, Lauren. You're a grown woman. You'll be starting a family of your own soon. You have your own life to lead, and so do I."

Lauren reached behind her and yanked her jacket off the back of the chair. "Okay, okay. Let's go and get this meeting over and done with."

Chapter Five

Lauren was relieved to see golden streaks of light burst through the sultry grey clouds. As far as she was concerned, there was nothing more depressing than being in London when the weather was miserable. She had always longed to live somewhere like L. A, where the sun always shone.

"How did you find this woman, Mum?" Lauren asked as they walked through the entrance of the modern glass building and waited for the lift.

"She worked for Mr. Reeves a couple of months ago. You remember him, right? The man whose wife swindled him for hundreds of thousands of pounds. Ms. Andrews traced it all to a labyrinth of accounts his wife had stashed it in, meaning he got a fair whack of it back."

"Oh, yeah, vaguely." Lauren sighed. "I'm glad things worked out okay for him."

"Me too."

The lift doors opened and they stepped in. Jean pressed the button to the first floor.

"Anyway," she continued. "I just happened to mention to Mr. Reeves that I had a financial leak, and he recommended her."

Lauren took a deep breath and slowly released it. There was no point in being antagonistic towards her mother. If she genuinely believed there was a mishap with the books, nothing Lauren said was going to change her mind. So maybe it was a good thing she had arranged to see an accountant – at least this expert with numbers would be able to put the matter to rest once and for all.

"Okay, well as long as you didn't mention Dad by name. You don't want him being the subject of gossip, especially if he hasn't done anything wrong."

"That's right, Lauren," she said with obvious exasperation. "Keep protecting your father at all costs. Don't worry about what this is doing to me."

Lauren rested her hand on her mother's arm and gave a gentle squeeze. "I'm sorry, Mum. I don't mean to be insensitive, but I really can't bear to think of the implications if Dad is involved with this."

Jean covered Lauren's hand with her own. "Oh, Lauren. Why won't you believe me when I tell you I'm not doing this to be malicious towards your dad. I'm hoping I'm wrong as much as you are."

The lift stopped and they stepped out onto a wide landing, the walls on either side decorated with large colourful abstract paintings.

Jean nodded her head in approval. "Someone's got taste." She looked to the right of her. "There's her office."

Lauren followed her mother's gaze and saw a dark brown sign with Andrews Accounting written in gold calligraphy. The door chimed when they entered and they stepped into a large airy room with a plush royal blue carpet. A chubby-cheeked receptionist looked up from her white iMac computer.

"Hello." She smiled. "Can I help you?"

"Yes," Jean said, "Jean Kellerman. We have an appointment with Ms. Andrews at eleven thirty."

"Oh, yes, you're the antiques people, aren't you?" the receptionist responded as she twirled a strand of hair around her finger. "I just love your shop. You have such beautiful furniture."

"Well, thank you," Jean said, smiling. "It's nice to see young people take an interest in antiques. Was there a piece you liked in particular?"

The receptionist's jaw dropped open, as her eyes darted around the room. "Um, well ... you know ... they're all nice."

Lauren gave a small shake of her head. She didn't have the patience for people who feigned interest in antiques like the woman had. She could always detect shallowness in people, and frankly, she found it boring and a drain of her energy to engage with them. *I bet Phoebe,* as Lauren had seen on the desk nameplate, *has never even passed by our shop, let alone come in.* Lauren sat down in the waiting area, leaving her mother at the desk, and picked up an old issue of Okay magazine.

Moments later, the phone on the large mahogany desk buzzed and was promptly picked up by Phoebe, who lifted her finger in the "just wait a minute" gesture to Jean. That was another pet hate of Lauren's. Was it really necessary? As if her mother had no social manners and would keep prattling on whilst the receptionist was talking to someone on the phone.

Lauren feigned a yawn and went back to reading

about rich, good-looking people with too much time on their hands.

"Ms. Andrews will see you now. Right this way," beamed Phoebe like she was about to take Lauren and her mother to meet the Prime Minister. Lauren rolled her eyes and put the magazine down.

Jean waited for her, and when Lauren was dutifully beside her, they started towards the door where Phoebe was standing, gesturing "this way," while still beaming. Lauren laughed quietly to herself. She would definitely last one day if her boss was not her mother. Maybe a half-day. It was the only friggin' door to go through, for crying out loud!

"This way?" asked Lauren with an innocent expression on her face as she approached Phoebe. Jean nudged her sharply. Her mother knew her too well, and Lauren smiled at her. When she looked through the open door, her heart practically jumped out of her chest.

Standing in front of them, shuffling papers behind her desk, was the woman – *the … woman … from … the … train.* Lauren stood frozen to the spot. She probably had the same expression as someone who'd recognised a fugitive serial killer.

Oh my God! This can't be happening!! Oh, but it was. Her mother walked up to the desk and glanced back at her paralysed daughter. Jean frowned at her and then turned back to Gillian Andrews.

"Good morning," she said warmly, looking up from her papers. "Gillian Andrews." She stood and extended her hand to Jean.

"So nice to meet you, Ms. Andrews …"

"Please, call me Gillian." She grinned.

"Okay, thank you, Gillian. I'm Jean Kellerman, and this is my daughter, Lauren." She looked back again at Lauren, who now seemed to have remembered how to walk and was moving forward.

Gillian laughed. "Well, well. Small world, Lauren."

Jean frowned in complete confusion and looked from Gillian back to her daughter, with a perplexed expression on her face.

"Do you two know each other?"

"Not really. We just happened to bump into each other on the train earlier this morning," Gillian said, smiling at Lauren.

"I'll tell you later, Mum. It's not a big deal." Lauren was glad that words were finally leaving her mouth.

See, it's like this, Mum. This is the woman I was fantasizing about this morning and ended up missing my stop for….

"Nice to meet you, Lauren," Gillian said extending her hand.

Her touch left Lauren flustered. "Likewise," she said and smiled back.

Gillian's hand enclosed hers, and with that smile and those eyes looking at her, Lauren felt that same jolt of electricity run through her that she experienced when she'd fantasized about their tryst at the hotel. What was it about this woman that gave her such a reaction?

Lauren's hand became clammy, and she instantly dropped it to her side. She wanted to wipe it on her jeans to dry it off but wasn't sure that would give a good impression.

"Please, take a seat," Gillian said.

Lauren and Jean looked at the two chairs in front of her desk and settled into them. Jean began to take papers out of the folder in her bag.

"I really appreciate you taking a look at these for me," Jean began. "This is not my area of expertise, by any means, but after my accountant spotted some irregularities, he suggested I hire someone to take a closer look. Like I told you on the phone, he thought that with the way the funds have been taken, trying to trace them is a little out of his depth."

"I totally understand your concerns, Mrs. Kellerman," Gillian said.

"Oh, Jean, please. I've highlighted where the anomalies are." Jean smiled warmly as she slid the paperwork across the desk.

"Ok, let's see what we've got here," Gillian stated quietly as she picked up the papers and started to flick through them.

Lauren could see Gillian's eyes reading rapidly, and her face took on a totally different expression of focus and concentration. She was trying her best not to stare, but she couldn't help but be intrigued by the woman. Gillian looked to be around twenty-five. Lauren was surprised to see there wasn't a wedding ring on her finger, and as she quickly scanned her desk and the rest of her minimalist office, she saw no pictures of husbands or children either.

Yes, well there's a wedding band on my finger, and a picture of Calum in my purse. She looked guiltily down at the beautiful engagement and wedding set that Calum had given her. *That's right, Calum – my husband. Whom I love and adore and am happily married to.* The last few words were thought without any amount of conviction. Who was she kidding? She wasn't happily married. If she were, surely she wouldn't be having fantasies about women, especially the woman sat right in front of her.

Gillian finally broke the silence and smiled. "Right, Mrs – I mean, Jean. Do you have the relevant invoices with you?"

"Of course. Here you go." Jean handed over the invoices she had been holding and waited patiently and silently as Gillian scanned them.

A slow smile spread across Lauren's face. Gillian's demeanour gave it away. She'd been right all along – her dad had done nothing wrong, she was sure he was in the clear.

With her mother looking out of the window and Gillian engrossed in the paperwork, Lauren flopped happily back in her seat; she had nothing more to worry about so she was free to study Gillian again. As she admired the way Gillian's sun-kissed hands slowly caressed the sheets of paper, she found herself completely mesmerised by the thought of Gillian's hands on her body. It wasn't long before her mind drifted off to fantasyland again.

She imagined herself sitting in her office, at her desk, restoring an old clock her mother had given her to work on…

There's a knock at the door. I look up, and it's Gillian. Her taut, rounded breasts strain against the tight fabric of her top, her nipples standing erect.

"Am I disturbing you?" she asks, hovering in the doorway.

"No, not at all. Please come in."

Gillian's eyes fall to the clock, and she smiles. "It's very beautiful," she says, nodding her head towards it.

"Yes it is – very beautiful." The words seem to get stuck in my throat as my eyes remain glued on hers. They are magnetic – pulling me in, daring me to lose myself in them.

She moves around to the side of my desk and sits on the edge, then leans in towards me and whispers, "Its beauty reminds me of you. Timeless."

I move my chair back a little to make more room. "You can touch it if you want." My words stumble over one another, but she doesn't seem to notice.

"Are you talking about the clock? Or you?" She rolls her tongue over the contours of her perfectly formed lips.

I can feel my heart start to beat faster, and I catch my breath. Gillian reaches down and takes my hands in her own. Holding them gently, she begins a slow, calming massage starting on the back of each hand with her strong thumbs. With soft circles, she works in ever increasing circumferences toward the tips of my fingers. She smiles knowingly as she notices the goose-

bumps exploding along my arms. My hands tremble, and she raises them to her mouth, sucking the tips of my fingers one by one. Molten shafts of desire burn its way through my veins. The sensation is both alien and exquisite.

"Do you like this?" she murmurs.

"Yes," I say breathlessly. Her mouth is hot and moist, making me wonder if she is as wet between her thighs.

"Stand up."

On weak legs, I stand, gripping her hands to steady me. They are warm, soft and confident. Her arms encircle me, drawing me against her. Every part of my body is moulded against hers. Her lips graze mine. I open my mouth waiting, yearning for her probing tongue to find mine – she's unleashed my hunger, now I want her to satisfy it.

I gasp when, without warning, her hand sears a path down my stomach and in between my thighs: feeling my nakedness, her fingers slip easily inside of me. With each deepening thrust, my nails dig deeper into her shoulders. Her eyes penetrate mine as if she can see into my soul. She remains watching me as I throw my head back and let out a stifled scream as my body feels like it's exploding into a million glowing stars. Every part of me is still throbbing as I bring my head forward to meet her gaze. I watch transfixed as she moves her hand up to her mouth and slowly licks her cum-slicked fingers with the tip of her tongue.

"I've been dreaming of tasting you from the very first time I laid eyes on you."

"I can see this is going to be an in-depth investigation. Usually in these cases I will need to come to your premises. Will that be ok?"

What?? What was that?? Lauren adjusted her eyes, as she glanced over at Gillian, trying to regroup her thoughts and get her brain functioning again.

"Lauren? Are you okay?" Her mother looked at her with a legitimate concern.

"Oh, I'm sorry," Lauren spluttered. "I had a late night," she said as an aside to Gillian as way of explanation. "My brain's half asleep."

Jean cleared her throat. "Let me see. I can get a member of staff to clear one of the offices that are being used for storage at the moment. I can have him put a desk and chair in there for you. He can probably have it ready for tomorrow if that's okay?"

"Tomorrow will be fine. I have a meeting in the morning, but I can come over in the afternoon." Gillian gathered the papers together and rested her hands on them.

"I'm sorry, Jean, but from what I've seen, it does look like there are some discrepancies," she said regretfully. "Once I've looked through the rest of your accounts, I'll have a better idea of what's going on. Does that sound alright?"

The muscles in Lauren's neck tautened and she rotated her head to loosen them. *This is not good news.* Lauren thought that this meeting would be the end of it. That Gillian would explain to her mother that it seemed like an honest mistake, and that would be the last she saw of her. Instead, Gillian had only confirmed her mother's worse fear – that someone had their sticky fingers in the till. Worse still, her mother was arranging for Gillian to come to the shop. *Hmm, maybe I'll just call in sick until she's finished with the books.*

"At least I'm not going mad or being paranoid." Jean shot a look at Lauren, then began to dig into her bag. "Do you want a payment for today?"

"No. This was a free consultation." Gillian opened her desk drawer and withdrew a leaflet. "These are my rates, if you want me to continue."

Jean took the leaflet and quickly scanned it. She looked up and nodded her head.

"Looks very reasonable. Just to let you know, my husband and I will be gone for a couple of days this week on business. We're opening a new office in Lancaster. But Lauren will be covering the shop. If you could liaise with her on this matter, that would be great."

Gillian glanced over at Lauren. "No problem at all. I'll be happy to let Lauren know my findings."

That's just great! Lauren had completely forgotten that her parents were leaving tomorrow. *That damn grand opening.* She saw her plan of taking time off go up in flames. *Either Calum is going to have the time of his life or if he isn't home, my vibrator is going to need new batteries.* She couldn't believe how sexually charged she felt right now. *Ok, horny. I feel horny. Just be honest. Being around this woman makes me want to rip her clothes off and…*

"If that's okay with you?" Gillian finished with a smile.

Lauren looked back at her. The heat of Gillian's gaze thrilled every one of her senses. "Yes, that's fine.

I'll see you tomorrow then."

"I look forward to it."

Gillian rose to her feet and shook hands with Lauren and Jean, before walking them to her office door. Lauren ambled behind her mother, and as she passed by Gillian, Gillian winked at her. *What? Did that just happen? Did she wink at me? Or did I imagine it?*

Once outside, Lauren was still questioning her eyesight as they made their way back to her mother's car.

"What an attractive woman. Did you notice she wasn't wearing a wedding band?" Jean said as she opened the car door and they got in.

"No, why would I?" Lauren said a little too quickly. "Besides, does it really matter that she isn't someone's wife? God forbid; we aren't in the Victorian era!" *At least I'm not delusional. Even Mum noticed how gorgeous she is.*

"Oh, come on." Jean laughed as she inserted the key and started the engine. "You've got to wonder what's wrong with her if she's that good looking and hasn't got a husband. Maybe she bats for the same team."

"I'm not having this conversation with you," Lauren said. She could only wonder what her mother knew about lesbians. She remained quiet for a few moments as she pulled the seatbelt across her chest. "Do you really think she could be a lesbian?"

Jean steered the car into the traffic. "You never know these days do you?"

Lauren burst out laughing at the thought of it. Gillian was about as much a lesbian as she was!

Chapter Six

Gillian sat on the edge of her desk and waited patiently for her call to be answered. After another two rings, Travis, her oldest friend, finally picked up.

"You're never going to guess what just happened."

"No, Gill. With you I can never guess what's going on in your life. Let me see – have you been skydiving again? Only this time, instead of breaking your leg, you've only grazed your knee. No, no wait, I know," he said eagerly. "You've decided you don't like the colour scheme in your apartment for the third time this year, and you've called the decorators in again."

Gillian chuckled. "None of the above."

"Don't tell me you're calling from the mud hut you lived in for three months when you ran away to Kenya last year."

"No, it's nothing so drastic. Did you get my email about the woman on the train this morning?"

She could hear him tapping his fingernail against the side of his phone. "Hmm, let me think. Are you talking about the email that sounded as if Danielle Steele herself had written it? If I recall, there was something about your heart fluttering. You've never felt this way before. Not being able to tear your eyes away from this goddess with piercing blue eyes and dark hair that never seemed to end – yeah, I read it. It was a good thing I wasn't eating breakfast because I'm sure I would have brought it all up."

"Ha ha, very funny."

He snorted. "No, I agree it wasn't. Anyway, what about her? Be quick. I'm trying to find an outfit for tonight that will make me look fabulous."

"That won't be too hard then. Where're you going?"

"To meet Cody's elderly mother."

Gillian eyed the seat Lauren had sat in only minutes ago and felt as if her stomach had been weighed down with an anchor. "Whoa, Travis, this really is getting serious isn't it? It's only been three months."

"I know, but love doesn't have a timeline. We have one life, sweetie, and I intend to use up every single minute of it. Anyway, enough about me, what were you saying about this hottie on the train?"

Gillian pushed herself off her desk and sat in Lauren's seat. She could still feel the warmth of Lauren's body heat. "She was just in my office."

"What! Are you kidding me?"

"Nope. I swear. She was with her mother," she said running her finger along the armrest.

"Ewwww, I don't think I want to hear any more about this. I'm as open-minded as the next person, but mothers and daughters don't float my boat."

Gillian laughed. "Get your mind out the gutter, Travis. This is what happens when there's too much access to free porn."

"I …"

"Yeah, I know, you don't watch it," she interjected

with humour.

"Well, I don't."

Gillian swung the chair from side to side feeling a little giddy. "Thou doth protest too much!"

Travis released a breath. "Okay, so if they weren't there for anything X-rated, why *were* they there?"

Gillian leaned her head back and stared up at the ceiling. "You know that antique shop in Kensington – the one you bought that beautiful dressing table from."

"The one that nearly bankrupted me. How could I forget?"

Gillian stopped swinging, stood up and strolled over to the window. "Well, they own it. It's a family business, and her mother wants me to look into their accounts."

Travis gave an exaggerated gasp. "What a strange coincidence. I told you it was only a matter of time before you met your one true love."

Gillian spotted Lauren and her mother as they walked towards a silver car and hopped in. "I don't think so," she said slowly as she watched the car mingle with the other traffic and disappear around a corner. "Unfortunately she has a wedding ring firmly welded to her finger and she seems a bit straight-laced."

"Really? That's what you said about what's-her-face Stella and look how she turned out – a nymphomaniac, psychopath on crack. No dear, after that episode I don't think you're the best person to judge someone's character, do you?"

She turned her back to the window and rested against it. Briefly closing her eyes, she tried to block out the memory. "When I'm reminded of her, no. But this one looks like Miss Prim and Proper. It's very endearing. Although I think she has some sort of attention deficiency."

Travis chuckled. "How so?"

"Well, on the train this morning she seemed to zone out. I was going to ask her if she was okay, but it didn't seem appropriate. Then in my office she did the same thing again. Even her mother looked a bit worried about her."

"Oh well, we've all got our crosses to bear, darling – some more than others."

"Yeah, I know. So shall we catch up tomorrow? I can't wait to hear how tonight goes at Cody's mum's."

"Of course, sweetie. We can people watch out your window with a bottle of wine."

"Sounds like a plan." That was one thing she loved about living in Soho – it was a doorway to London's buzzing nightlife.

"Listen, Gill, on a serious note, don't invite any more trouble into your life. You really don't need the drama."

"I know, I know." She sighed. "Nothing ever come of it, but a girl is allowed to dream, isn't she?"

"As long as it stays firmly in your brain and nowhere else, then yes. But I know what you're like. Any sign of encouragement and you think it's all there for the taking."

"No, Travis. I think I've learnt my lesson, believe me."

"Good. Well, I'd better shoot off. Until tomorrow, my love," he said blowing her a kiss down the phone.

"Can't wait." Gillian disconnected the call, then walked around her desk and took a seat.

Travis was right; it was a mad coincidence. It was also a shame that the only woman to catch her eye in a long time just happened to be married and straight.

Chapter Seven

Unable to keep thoughts of Gillian out of her mind for more than five minutes at a time, Lauren did the only thing she could – kept busy. She spent the day going through the backlog of invoices she'd been putting off for the past few weeks. As well as getting instructions from her mother on what needed to be finished and delivered while they were away. Whilst her dad had every confidence in her ability to handle the business by herself for a couple of days, her mother, as usual, had her doubts.

"Maybe I should just stay," Jean said, after going over the details yet again.

"Jean! It's our grand opening. You have to be there," Ken protested, tugging at his tie in frustration.

Lauren let out a heavy sigh. "Mum. Seriously, I've got this. Worst-case scenario, if there're any problems, I'll tell some customers they'll have to wait a couple more days until you get back. They'll understand."

Jean considered this. "Okay, I just feel bad since we are kind of busy, but I guess that can't be helped. And I don't want to keep you from being at home. I know you and Calum don't have much time together right now as it is."

Lauren rolled her eyes. "Mum, it's a couple of days. Stop being so dramatic."

The door to the adjoining workshop opened, and a stocky man dressed in a dark blue overall filled the doorway. "Mrs. Kellerman, I've cleared the office – I'll give it a good clean before I leave tonight and it should be ready for use."

"Thank you, Tyler," Jean said kindly.

"Yes, thanks," Lauren added. "Don't worry about cleaning it. I'll do it myself in a minute. That chest you're working on needs to be finished. Mrs Springer's been on the phone fretting about it being delivered on time."

"Whatever you say boss," he said before retreating to the workshop.

"We'd better be off, love. We've still got packing to do," Ken said as he neared the shop's entrance.

Lauren saw a look of disdain flash over her mother's features. *The sooner Gillian finds out that Dad's done nothing wrong, the sooner Mum and Dad can repair their relationship. Honestly, Dad having an affair! Whatever will she think of next?*

She walked her mum to the door. "Don't worry about anything. Just have a good time," she said, closing the door behind them.

Right, what to do now? Shopping for tonight's dinner. She made a mental note to pick up a few ready-made meals from Marks and Spencer's – not even she fancied eating her own horrid concoctions tonight.

She checked her phone for messages. She hadn't heard from Calum all day, which was not unusual. He never knew what his schedule was going to be, and Lauren had understood this before she married him. She could not imagine having such a stressful job. He worked sixteen hours most days. Yes, it was because he was a trainee but still, she doubted that would change even when he qualified. She couldn't expect him to say to a patient, "Um, sorry, yes I know you're dying, but I must dash, my wife's got dinner in the oven."

No, he would never say that. They'd cope somehow. They always had. As she walked to her office, she finally relented and let Gillian slip back into her thoughts. Lauren knew her mum was being judgmental, but had she been right with her observations – was Gillian single? No wedding ring didn't mean no boyfriend. *There must be loads of men beating down a path to her door.*

Later that evening when Lauren carried her shopping bags through her front door, thoughts of Gillian still lingered in her mind. *Do I fancy her? I can't!* What would that say about her if she did? She couldn't turn into a lesbian overnight. *Could I?* She chastised herself. Of course, she couldn't. She was as straight as … Gillian. It was only natural to admire someone's beauty; she did it all the time with the people that passed through the shop. *But you don't want to have sex with them do you?* she reminded herself. *It must be that time of the month when my hormones are all over the place.*

She set the shopping down on the worktop, then started to unpack and put the food in the fridge.

"Hello, my little angel. Have you missed me?" she said as Scruff trotted towards her, his small body brushing against her leg. She bent down and scooped the wriggling dog into her arms.

"How about a kiss?" she said dropping one on his head.

Hearing her phone vibrate, she set Scruff down and withdrew it from her pocket.

Her eyes widened when she flipped it open and read the message.

Hi! Your mum gave me your number. Hope that's ok. Just wanted to let you know I'll be with you around 9am tomorrow. My meeting was cancelled. It must have been fate this morning; maybe our destinies are on a collision course. Ha ha. Gillian.

The message left her dumbfounded. *It's a text. It doesn't mean anything.* Then why did she hope it was a cryptic message and Gillian was secretly trying to tell her something? Maybe it was because her heart had skipped a beat when she realised who the message was from.

Should I reply? She glanced at the time on her phone. There was no need to she concluded. It wasn't as if Gillian had asked a question. *But won't it be rude not to acknowledge the message with an okay?* The internal debate raged on. *Why does this woman make it impossible for me to think straight?* She smiled to herself. The pun wasn't lost on her.

Scruff's sudden bark broke her mental dithering.

"Okay, I know, baby. You want to go walkies," she said as she took him into the hallway and slipped on his lead.

Fortunately, since his legs measured about four

inches, it never took that long for Scruff to get his exercise in for the day. While she waited by a tree for him to finish sniffing, she pulled her phone out of her pocket and re-read the message.

Okay. I'm going to do it. I don't want her to think I've got no manners. Just be professional and casual, she told herself as she tapped in the message.

Hi. Thanks for letting me know. See you then.

Send. Okay. There, she'd done it. She re-read the message she'd just sent. It was fine. If Calum happened to read it, there was nothing inappropriate to be seen. Now, if he happened to read her mind, that would be something else. Thank God she hadn't married a psychic.

A second later her phone vibrated again. She hesitated. Her fingers trembled. *This can't be healthy.* She hit the unlock screen.

Hi Babe – Home in an hour!!!!

Swallowing her disappointment like a bitter pill, Lauren felt like the Wicked Witch of the East. Here she was feeling aggrieved the message hadn't come from a woman she barely knew, while her loyal husband was excited to be on his way home to her; his emotionally unfaithful wife. *You need to get your act together girlie and quick.* When she returned home she left her phone in the kitchen, with the intention of forgetting about Gillian and getting ready to blow Calum's mind.

An hour later, Lauren heard the front door open and Scruff barking.

"Hey, honey, I'm home," Calum called out.

Lauren didn't answer. She lay still and waited on their bed.

"Lauren?" he called again.

She heard his footsteps sprinting up the stairs, then along the landing to the closed bedroom door. When the door opened, she heard him gasp, and she smiled to herself. Candles lit the room, and classical music softly played in the background. Only the flickering light of the candles illuminated her naked body splayed out on the bed waiting for him.

"Well, hello!" he said and moved towards the bed. He was unbuckling his belt as she grabbed him and pulled him down on top of her.

"I missed you," she whispered in his ear as his mouth searched for hers.

Lauren closed her eyes and as hard as she tried, she couldn't rid the image of Gillian from her mind.

My soul is awoken by the feel of moist lips moving along the base of my neck. Ripples of pleasure course through me as her hand moulds to the firm swell of my breast.

She moves her mouth to my ear. "Do you want me?" Gillian's voice is nothing more than a seductive whisper.

I don't answer. Instead, I cup her cheek with my palm. The sweet scent of vanilla emanates from her hair, as I draw her face closer. Her lips are soft against mine as I open my mouth, and her tongue sweeps inside without any hesitation. My hands lock behind her head as our kiss deepens. The heat between us is intense as she spreads my legs open with her own, wedging them firmly between mine. I can feel my juices coating her thigh as she rubs her strong, unyielding muscle against my throbbing clit.

Her mouth lingers on mine before she breaks the kiss. As I arch my head back into the softness of the pillow, she ducks her head, seizing my nipple in her mouth, pulling and suckling at the pebbled peak as I squirm wantonly against her leg.

The feel of her mouth clamped on my breast sends spasms straight to my core. She slips her hand between our sweat slicked bodies and finds my entrance. Her body heat scorches me as she massages my swollen nub of flesh. I press down hard as she curves two fingers into me. My muscles constrict as she thrusts them in and out of my passage, and I cry out, "Harder," breathlessly in her ear.

Our bodies thrash about on the silk sheets like we are caught up in a full-blown gale. I'm too dizzy and light-headed with desire to care what we look like. One more thrust and I feel my floodgates open as the muscles in my passage clamp around her fingers. Her body tenses then relaxes.

Her tongue is inside my mouth again, only this time it moves with urgency. Her kiss is as intoxicating as fine wine. She moves on top of me, and I grip both her bum cheeks, pulling her tight against me as I slip and slide, riding her leg. I grind against her until I find myself gulping for air as bolts of pleasure come in rapid succession.

"Whoa, what's got into you," Calum said, rolling off Lauren and onto his back.

Lauren slid naked from the bed. She clamped her mouth shut to imprison the sobs that threatened to break free. "I'm going to take a quick shower before I start dinner," she said in a strangled voice.

"Hey." Calum's eyes clouded over with concern as he pushed himself up into a sitting position. "Is there something wrong?"

She kept her face to the door as she brushed away a tear. "Not at all. I'm just feeling a bit emotional. I think I'm due on."

"Are you sure?"

"Yes," she said as a twinge of guilt settled in her mind.

"Is there anything I can do for you?"

As he swung his legs off the bed she turned and raised her hand. In a panicked voice she said, "No, no, stay put and rest. I won't be a minute." Fumbling with the door handle she pushed it open and disappeared behind the door, slowly crumpling to the floor. No amount of regret could wash away the tide of shame she felt at that moment in time. She vowed she would never think about Gillian again. The survival of her marriage depended on it.

Chapter Eight

Lauren lay in the stillness of the night, her mind racked with guilt. She couldn't believe how intense that fantasy had been about Gillian. She had not thought of Calum once throughout the whole time. Every touch and every stroke she imagined Gillian's hand delivering it. She couldn't look Calum in the eye afterwards; self-conscious that he would see her desire had been aroused – not by him – but a mere stranger.

Lauren took a long leisurely bath so by the time she left the bathroom, she knew Calum would have fallen asleep. She leaned over and ran the tip of her finger along the stubble on his chiselled jaw. *Even in his sleep he looks exhausted.* He worked so hard to make her happy in every area of her life, why couldn't he reach her emotionally, where it mattered most. Instead of being at one with him when they made love, she was busy thinking about a woman she barely knew. *Because it's not right between Calum and I any more, and the worst thing is, I don't know whether it ever really was. The sex is okay,* she admitted to herself. *But it's not like it should be. I shouldn't have to be thinking about a woman to get any kind of pleasure.*

The evening of playing the "hot and horny wife", wasn't the first time Lauren had tried to *fix* things. But in the end, once Calum had climbed on top of her, it was the same routine, same style, same time frame. *The same lack of connection.*

Lauren sighed. She was torn between what her mind thought was the best path for her to follow and what her heart needed to function properly. She knew that if she was feeling unsatisfied, she needed to figure out why and talk to Calum. Not about the fantasies. That would be stupid. No, they needed to talk about their relationship and where it was going. *And exactly when will he have time for that conversation? Or the energy?* She could picture that scene in her mind. The "Let's talk" conversation would have him running for the hills. Maybe that was the problem – they were both burying their heads in the sand and neither of them wanted to face the truth. The truth being that something was broken, and she didn't know if the relationship was strong enough to fix it. Maybe she was overthinking and worrying about it too much? *Damn, maybe I'm turning into my mother.*

Lauren reached over to the white wicker chair beside the bed and pulled her dressing gown towards her. Standing, she slipped into it, taking one last look at Calum before heading down to the kitchen.

She thought about finishing up the bottle of wine she'd opened earlier. Glancing at the clock, she saw that it was almost midnight. *Well, why not? It's not like I'm employee of the year or anything?* Then she remembered, her parents were away and she needed to be on time to open the shop. The wine stayed in the fridge, and she opted for a mug of milky hot chocolate instead. On the kitchen table, she noticed her phone blinking. Picking it up, she saw she had a message.

Looking forward to working with you – who knows where it will lead!

Gillian had replied to her text. What was it with her cryptic messages? Was she attracted to Lauren, or just a natural flirt? Lauren couldn't understand why temptation was always put in front of her when she was at her most vulnerable. She was at a crossroads in her life and didn't know what she wanted, and even if she did, she doubted she'd have the strength to follow her convictions.

Lauren sat with the phone in her hand until she had finished her drink, trying her hardest to control her thoughts. What was the point of getting herself in a state over something that was never going to happen?

Rather than go back to bed she made her way through to the living room and lay down on the sofa. After much tossing and turning, with wild anticipation about seeing Gillian the following morning, she fell asleep.

***

The next morning Lauren was awoken by the feel of a cold nose and a soft tongue on her lips.

Where she was lying, her face had been in perfect range for a smooch.

"Ewwww … Scruff!" she said, wiping her face with the back of her hand.

Oh why couldn't he have let me sleep for another ten minutes? Lauren had been dreaming about Gillian. She couldn't remember exactly what had happened, but judging by how randy she felt she could well imagine. Scruff stared at her with his soulful brown eyes. He was up on his hind legs, his tail wagging manically as she stroked his head.

"You are so damn cute, I forgive you," Lauren said as she pulled him up on the sofa with her. She grabbed her phone off the coffee table and glanced at the time. It was 7:00 am. Calum was going to be up any minute. The coffee pot had auto brewed at 6:45 and the scent in the air was heavenly. She just had to find the energy to get up and pour herself a cup.

Calum's footsteps stomped down the stairs. Within seconds, he was standing in the doorway, wearing a pair of tracksuit bottoms.

"Hey, babe. Why are you on the sofa?"

With a sigh of fatigue, Lauren stretched out her legs. "I was feeling restless."

"You should have woken me." He grinned, walking over to her and kissing the top of her head. "I could have easily gone another round."

Lauren glanced toward the window, through which the morning light was streaming in, and wished she had closed the blind the previous night. She just wanted to roll over and go back to sleep, but instead pushed herself up onto her elbows. "I doubt it, Cal. World War Three couldn't have woken you up last night," Lauren said, dryly.

"Well, I'm awake now."

Why did he always want sex in the morning?

How could she possibly have married a morning person? "I have to open up the shop today, I'm afraid."

"Where are your mum and dad?"

"Gone for a couple of days. They're opening a new shop in Lancaster."

"Oh well. At least you'll have some peace and quiet."

Lauren nodded, her eyes following him as he left the room.

"Coffee?" he called out from the kitchen.

"Yes, please," she said as she picked Scruff up and put him on the floor. She needed to shower and get dressed before Calum decided to join her and continue what she'd started last night. Until she could sort out the reason for her fantasies about Gillian, she'd decided that sex with Calum was going to be off the menu. She needed to get to the bottom of her angst, even if it meant facing up to a part of herself that she never knew existed.

Chapter Nine

Lauren arrived at work at 8:30am on the dot. She was shocked to realise it was the earliest she'd ever been there. Unlocking the front door, she headed straight to her office, letting Scruff off the lead, who immediately went on the hunt for his stuffed rabbit. Finding it under Lauren's desk, Scruff bounded onto his bed and began chewing on an ear.

"You're a funny one aren't you?" Lauren laughed. "Now I want you to be good for five minutes. Mummy is going on a coffee run."

Since she'd made good time this morning, Lauren decided she would go to the coffee shop on the street corner and pick up a latte and a muffin or two.

The air in the small, quaint shop was heavily laden with odours that made Lauren's stomach growl as she walked in. There was nothing like the smell of good rich coffee and fresh baked goods to make even a non-morning person like Lauren glad to be up. She stood in line, flipping through the news headlines on her phone when she heard a familiar voice behind her.

"Are you stalking me?"

Turning, Lauren saw Gillian standing in front of her. She was dressed similarly to the day before – blue jeans and a black leather jacket. Gillian grinned at her, and she smiled back.

Lauren's stomach was in knots, but at least her mouth worked. "Well, since I got here first, I would suggest the opposite," she replied feeling the heat gather in her cheeks.

"Ah yes. I suppose you're right. Good thing I'm not a detective," she said with a raised brow.

Lauren laughed. Even first thing in the morning and up close she was so unbelievably sexy.

"I nearly didn't recognise you with your hair down," Gillian said, gently reaching out and touching a strand of Lauren's hair.

Lauren unconsciously stepped back and laughed nervously. Gillian had obviously noticed she'd made an effort with her appearance this morning. Searching her mind for a response, she blurted out, "Yes, my husband prefers my hair down."

Gillian smiled. "He has good taste."

Is she flirting with me? It sure sounded like it. Seriously, how could this woman be flirting with her, right there in the middle of a coffee shop, in broad daylight?

Lauren watched in a daze as Gillian's tongue swept across her perfectly formed lips, and a rush of heat flushed through her whole body.

Oblivious to the effect she was having on her, Gillian clasped her hands together. "Hey, listen. I know it is kind of off the cuff, but I'm not going to get through half of the files before midday. Shall we go out for lunch? I hate eating alone."

Lauren hesitated. She had the shop and Scruff to watch over. "Um, well …"

"Think of it as a business lunch. You can bill me

if that makes you feel better," Gillian joked.

Lauren shuffled slightly on her feet. "I'm sorry; I can't. It's just with my parents gone; I'm in charge of the shop. And I have Scruff with me too."

Gillian looked puzzled. "Scruff?"

Lauren's hand flew to her mouth as she giggled. "Oh, yeah, sorry, he's our miniature dachshund." *That's right "our" as in mine and Calum's, my husband Calum*, she reminded herself.

Gillian didn't skip a beat. "Okay, then how about I grab a couple of sandwiches and we can eat in your office or my temporary one. Whichever suits you best?"

Wow, this woman doesn't let up. Lauren paused before responding. She didn't want to come across as being rude. But lunch with this woman, wasn't that crossing a fine line? All she wanted was for Gillian to look at the accounts, confirm her father had done nothing wrong and get the hell out of both her mind and life. What she didn't want was to get to know her any better. Who knew what would come of it?

"Hmmmm … ermmmmm." *Just say no! It's only a two letter word.* Instead, she heard herself saying, "Alright, if it won't be too much trouble. That sounds good."

Gillian beamed. "Fantastic. Thank you."

"No, thank you. You're the one making all the effort."

"Oh, it's my pleasure, believe me."

Lauren remained quiet as she examined Gillian's

features studiously, unable to tear her eyes away.

"Next."

The sound of the server's voice broke the moment. It was Lauren's turn at the counter. She gave her order and turned back to Gillian after receiving her food and drink.

"I would wait for you but I'd better get back, God knows what Scruff is getting up to," she said with a nervous laugh. "I'll see you in a little while."

"You sure will," Gillian said, grinning broadly.

Lauren's hold on the muffin bag tightened as she walked past her. Once out on the street, she took a deep breath. What was it about that woman? She was too good to be true; Thoughtful, playful. She was also a little forward.

"That's not really a positive quality," Lauren mumbled to herself as she walked back towards the shop. *Maybe I'm totally off track and just wishing she was flirting with me.*

"This is going to send me loopy in the end," she said to herself, as she dodged people, fiercely protecting her coffee like it was the Crown Jewels. *Look at me; I'm talking to myself already.* If she was this rattled after only three interactions with her, she dreaded to think what she'd be like by the time Gillian finished going through the books

.

Chapter Ten

You stupid fool! What's wrong with you? Gillian gave a slight shake of her head as she replayed the last few minutes in her head. What had she been thinking coming on to Lauren so strong? Why had she put her in such an uncomfortable position? She could tell Lauren didn't want to have lunch with her, but she had pushed on and on like some sort of desperado. She hadn't missed Lauren emphasising the existence of her husband when talking about their dog. Gillian had been looking forward to today but after this episode, she wasn't so sure. Maybe she should have asked Mrs. Kellerman to have the boxes of files delivered to her office, which really was her normal procedure. But no, she just couldn't resist the temptation of getting to know Lauren a little bit better.

Maybe Travis was right in his assessment of her – she was always attracted to women who were out of her reach. It was hard meeting a soul mate if you weren't on the gay scene. She had the occasional drink at Robin's bar but that's as far as it went nowadays. The gay scene was too complicated for her. She liked her relationships to be straightforward with no drama. But just because that's what she preferred didn't mean that's what she got. In her five years of actively dating, she had only met one woman who had been a suitable match and what do you know – she turned out to be married.

Maybe it was her destiny to be alone. Travis thought she'd set her standards too high when it came to finding the love of her life. Gillian disagreed. She wasn't overly fussy but she wasn't going to settle for someone just for the sake of it. She had seen too many relationships fall to the wayside because people had just jumped right in without any real thought. No, she'd rather wait and if no one came along, so be it.

"One hot chocolate, double cream and marshmallows," the server said as he held out the drink to her.

"Thank you," Gillian said, taking the cup from him with a smile.

She couldn't wait to get stuck in. Chocolate was her one weakness. *Well, that and married women apparently.* Thankfully, no matter how much she ate, she managed to keep the weight off. It was a godsend. Both her parents were still very slim, despite not doing much in the way of exercise due to having desk jobs.

Exiting the coffee shop, Gillian sat down on the bench outside to finish her drink. She'd wait ten minutes to give Lauren time to open up and get things in order. Checking her phone messages, she frowned. Travis hadn't been in touch yet, which was surprising considering she'd normally receive at least ten text messages as he went about his morning. She thought he would have been itching to give her the details from his evening at Cody's mum's the night before.

Oh well, he's obviously enjoying himself, whatever he's doing. Pushing thoughts of Travis aside, Gillian focused on what she had to do next. *You're going to go into that shop and do your job, and leave the poor woman alone.* That was going to be a tough call though. She still couldn't figure out what exactly it was that drew her to Lauren. Yes, she was attractive, but so were lots of other women. Yet she'd never felt this way about any of them, *except one.*

Her thoughts pressed on. Was the attraction down to Lauren being attached? Was it the challenge? No, that was armchair psychology babble. She could never understand that theory. Why on earth would anyone deliberately go after something they could never have? Maybe her attraction was just one of those natural phenomena without any rational rhyme or reason. *It just is what it is,* she tried to convince herself. But as she stood and began walking towards the antique shop, she knew there had to be more to meeting Lauren than just a coincidence. She truly believed everything happened for a reason and despite herself, she felt the excitement mounting in her at the thought of spending more time with Lauren.

Chapter Eleven

Lauren reached the shop and set down her coffee on the step before unlocking the door. Her heart had finally resumed its normal pace after her unexpected encounter with Gillian. She glanced at her watch; it was just before 9:00. Lucy, their sales assistant, would be arriving soon, leaving her to get on with work in the back. The "fierce and mighty" Scruff barked madly on the other side of the door when he heard her key in the lock.

"Shhh, Scruff, you'll wake the dead at this rate," Lauren hissed. Pushing the door open, Scruff ran out and jumped up on her like he hadn't seen her in years.

"Okay, boy. Mummy's here," she said smiling as she patted his head. Dropping onto all fours, he did a three-sixty turn, lifted his leg and let out a squirt of pee right next to her coffee cup.

"Scruff! Oh my God, really?" Lauren snatched up her coffee before it either got completely peed on or knocked over. Flipping the lights on in the shop with her elbow, she hurried to her office, grabbed the mop that was kept in the cupboard, and went back to the front step to clean up Scruff's welcome present.

She covered the yellow puddle with the mop and rinsed it out in the bucket. *I don't care what Calum says, this dog has issues.* She was thankful for small mercies. Scruff was only a small dog. She dreaded to think how much pee a ten stone St. Bernard could unleash. *I guess that puts my little puddle back into perspective.* Lauren laughed out loud at the thought.

She flipped the sign on the door to open, and after rinsing out the mop and bucket, returned them to the cupboard.

"Has Scruff been up to no good again?" Lucy said laughing as she walked through the front door.

Lauren joined in with the laughter. "Yep. Two more inches and I'd be drinking his pee instead of coffee."

"He's adorable though isn't he?"

"He is that. Are you okay out here by yourself today?"

"Sure."

"Okay, I'll see you in a bit." Lauren started to make her way to her office, and then stopped abruptly before briefly turning around. "Oh, I forgot to say, I'm expecting someone in a little while, just ask her to wait here and I'll come and get her."

"Okay."

Entering her office, Lauren switched on the answering machine and listened to the messages that had been left since the previous day. Most were either requesting estimates or wanting status updates. Her mum had even left her a "Good morning, I hope you're not going to arrive at midday" message. Lauren rolled her eyes. She would always be unreliable to her mother. Always daddy's little girl. Deep down, Lauren was fine with that.

She knew she shouldn't complain. Her mother

was like an angel compared to Calum's, and that was saying something. His parents lived in Mayfair and were both already retired at the grand old age of fifty, due to his dad striking gold in the property development boom. Now they spent their time jet-setting around the world or having weekend long parties for their ilk.

She knew they didn't really approve of her. They were polite, not friendly. She usually got the impression that they felt their son had "settled" by marrying her.

Once, she had tried to talk to Calum about it, but he had dismissed her concerns with his usual mantra. "They'll come around, just give them time."

She had been brown-nosing them for eight years to no avail. So she had become more proactive and now refused to have much to do with them; only seeing them at special gatherings like christenings or milestone birthdays.

Lauren sat back in her chair and looked at her callback list. She wasn't in the mood to listen to customers telling her, probably made up stories, about how their antique desk was used by Queen Victoria or their precious chair had King George's bum imprint still on it.

She never really understood the antiques business, which was strangely ironic considering that the business fed and clothed her family. Lauren just saw old things that needed to be replaced. *Maybe I'm just shallow and have no appreciation for culture and history. Or maybe I just like my stuff new. Nothing wrong with that either.* She did admit that some older items had more creative designs and intricacy than modern desks or tables. But in the end, you just needed something to write or sit on. Did it really matter if it was a hundred years old?

The chime from the shop door opening jolted her out of her daydream. "Scruff, she's here."

Scruff looked up at her totally disinterested, and then returned to gnawing the bottom of her chair.

"Okay, keep calm," she told herself as she combed back her hair with her fingers and hurried out of the room.

As Lauren reached the open door that led into the showroom, she refrained from stepping inside. Instead, she drew to a slow stop and rested against the wall. Her eyes wandered over Gillian's thick, glossy hair dangling in midair as she bent over a piece of furniture. Lauren took a sharp intake of breath as her eyes followed Gillian's finger which slowly traced the edge of a desk. Lauren's eyelids fluttered as she fought the imagery that was making its way to the forefront of her mind. She had promised herself she wouldn't do it any more. A sigh escaped her lips as her mind drifted.

She had to get control over this. She couldn't keep doing this … could she?

I'm waiting next to the lift to go up to the first floor of the shopping centre. Out of nowhere Gillian appears beside me. Her eyes dance with mischief as she wraps her arm around my waist and pulls me close.

"*Surprised to see me?*" *A small smile twists her red-coated lips.*

I nod dumbfounded. I'm surprised but elated at the same time.

Suddenly, she pushes me against the wall, and I can feel the roughness of the surface graze my skin, but I ignore the pain. I am heady with anticipation of what she'll do next. She doesn't care people are watching us as they make their way to their cars – she seems to relish us being on show. She presses her mouth against mine and slides her tongue between my lips. At the feel of her hot probing tongue entwining with mine, spikes of desire arouse in me. I can feel the heat growing between my thighs as her hand snakes between my legs and presses against my throbbing clit. I notice people are no longer just looking at us and going on their way, they are stopping to stare. I can feel my cheeks flushing in embarrassment but as much as I want her to stop, my body yearns for her touch; for her to release my pent up desire.

Breathlessly, Gillian pulls her mouth slightly away, her eyes hold me captive. "Do you want me to fuck you with all these people watching us? Is that what you want?"

My breath comes out in short sharp gasps as I say through gritted teeth. "Yes!" With a sense of urgency, I reach under my skirt and pull aside my underwear, guiding her fingers to lose themselves in my wetness.

Chapter Twelve

"Oh, sorry I didn't see you standing there. I was just admiring this desk."

Lauren jumped back as if someone had just thrown a bucket of ice-cold water over her. Her eyes darted to Lucy, who was carrying a clock through to the next room.

Gillian eyed Lauren with concern. "Hey, are you okay?" she asked, moving towards her.

Lauren held up a hand as she stumbled backwards. "Yes. Sorry, I'm … I'm fine," she said more sharply than she intended. She was on the edge of panic. Had she mumbled anything while in the midst of her fantasy?

Gillian tilted her head to the side. "You don't look fine to me. Your face is beetroot red." She glanced around the room. "Can I get you a glass of water or something?"

Lauren smiled faintly. She had never felt so embarrassed in her life. All she wanted to do was bury her face in her hands. "No, honestly, I'm okay. It's just a bit hot in here," she said fanning herself with her hand, trying to regain her composure.

Gillian eyed her quizzically but said nothing. Lauren was grateful for her discretion. The room was anything but hot. By the way Gillian was looking at her; Lauren wouldn't have been surprised if Gillian thought she was as nutty as a fruitcake.

"Okay. If you're sure." Gillian looked away from her towards the desk she'd been inspecting. "As I was saying, this is a beautiful piece."

"Do you think so? If I'm honest, I'm more of an Ikea girl myself," Lauren blurted out before she could stop herself. *Oh that's just great! Make yourself look even more of an idiot.*

Gillian gazed at her with eyes she found herself wanting to get lost in. Lauren had never been an eye person and, if pressed, she couldn't even remember what colour her dad's eyes were. She only remembered Calum's because he was always telling her that the nurses at the hospital said he had beautiful blue eyes.

Gillian smiled at her. Lauren was relieved to see it was genuine – not a half-arsed patronising grin that some of the customers gave her sometimes. Nevertheless, she still wished she would have kept her mouth shut. What was that saying her mother loved to quote? "Better to remain silent and be thought a fool than to speak out and remove all doubt."

"Nothing wrong with honesty, Lauren. Imagine how different the world would be if we all said what was really on our minds."

Lauren swallowed hard. *Was that a challenge?* But a challenge to do what? To tell Gillian she had been fantasizing about her like a pubescent teenager. Had Gillian realised there was something amiss every time they were in close contact? *Surely not, unless I'm emitting more signals than I'd imagined.*

Lauren cleared her throat. "I don't know if I

agree with that, sometimes maybe but not always," she said switching her thoughts to her mother's predicament. If her dad really was cheating on her, finding out the truth would break her heart.

"You sound like you're speaking from experience."

Lauren smiled. There was no way she was going to let her guard down and start airing her family's dirty laundry to Gillian. If she did that, what would she do next – start telling her about her own marriage problems? Instead of responding to Gillian's comment she put on her cool professional tone.

"You must be itching to take a look at the books." She turned swiftly and gestured for Gillian to follow. "All the files are in the boxes; my office is here." Lauren nodded her head towards her office door as they passed it. "If you need anything, just give me a shout," she said reaching for the door handle and pushing open the door to the office Gillian would be using.

"Thank you."

Lauren smiled and retreated to her own office. Once inside, she flopped onto her leather office chair and propped her elbows on the desk.

She looked down at the phone and considered calling her mum and asking her to return early. No, that would be a bad idea. Instead, she said a silent prayer that Gillian would be so caught up in paperwork all day that she wouldn't have to see her again. The feelings Gillian elicited in her were criminal.

Her heart skipped a beat when she heard a tap at

her door. *Oh God, I don't know how much more my heart can take.* She braced herself to see Gillian appear in the doorway.

"Come in."

The door slowly opened and Lucy stepped in carrying a parcel.

Lauren smiled, not knowing whether she was disappointed or relieved. She recognised the discrete packaging, it was from Ann Summers. Calum had obviously thought she deserved some lingerie.

"Package for your dad," Lucy said handing it to her.

It took several seconds for the words to register as she took the parcel. "For my dad?"

"Yep. Well, at least that's who it's addressed to."

Lauren frowned as she looked down at the addressee. "Thanks, Lucy."

Lucy left the office. Lauren turned the parcel over in her hand. Was this for her mother or for her father's other woman? She didn't want to think about it. Her father … cheating. She inhaled deeply. *Okay, now slow down and cool your jets. This could all be very innocent. It may well be a present for Mum. So much for defending him. I'm worse than Mum for jumping to conclusions.*

She tossed the package on the window sill. Before she made any judgments, she'd wait for her dad to come home and see what he had to say for himself. For now, she needed to get on with her work.

Chapter Thirteen

The morning whizzed by, and Lauren thought it was a little busier than usual for a Tuesday. Within three hours, she had talked to four potential new customers and had given status updates on six other ongoing projects.

At the sound of a knock on the door, Scruff jumped out of his basket and ran towards it, barking like he was a Rottweiler. Her Dad had wanted to put a "Beware of the Dog" sign out front, but her mother thought that would be bad for business. *What mother wants mother usually gets.*

She glanced at her watch. 12:00. "Come in," she called out.

"Hey! Whoa there, killer!" Lauren heard that soft, sexy voice as Gillian walked in.

"Scruff!" Lauren said.

Gillian bent over and petted Scruff, who instantly stopped barking. He stood on his hind legs leaning against Gillian, his tail wagging ecstatically, and then, without warning, he peed on her boot.

"Whoa," Gillian jumped back.

Lauren's hand covered her mouth. "Oh my God! I'm so sorry. The vet says it's a nervous thing. He only does it when he gets really excited."

Gillian laughed. "I think he's the smartest dog I've ever met. He knows he's not that big, so he gets you close and then he lets loose. Pretty smart if you ask me."

"Well, I'm sorry. I should have warned you. I keep waiting for the day he outgrows it. Do you want me to wash your boot?"

"Nah, don't worry about it. I think he mostly missed. He sure is cute." Gillian bent over to pet him again. "A little puppy pee never hurt anyone, did it killer?"

Lauren had an irrational feeling of jealousy towards Scruff. It took her a minute to realise that it was because she wished she were being petted by Gillian instead. Hell, she'd happily pee on her boot, though she didn't think Gillian would find that as cute.

Gillian reached into the oversized bag slung over her shoulder and withdrew a large paper bag. So, she had obviously already picked up lunch. Lauren didn't know whether to feel touched or annoyed that Gillian had just presumed she knew her taste in food without asking. If it had been Calum she would have seen it as a sweet gesture, but from Gillian, it was just another step into her private space. *Maybe she doesn't even realise it, or maybe she does and just doesn't care.* Calum had accused her of being able to put a negative spin on Santa Claus' motives if she thought about it long enough. He was right. Lauren did over-think most things. Ok, almost everything. But what was the harm in that? It wasn't her fault she had an analytical mind.

"I hope you don't mind, but I took the liberty of choosing something I thought you'd like."

Lauren forced a smile as she stood up to clear her

desk and make space. "No, not at all. I like surprises," she lied.

"Good. That's just what I thought."

Okay, let's see what you've got then, mystic Meg. Gillian was too overly confident for Lauren's liking and she couldn't wait to take her down a peg or two when she turned her nose up at her offerings. She soon changed her tune when Gillian pulled the sandwiches out of the bag and laid hers in front of her.

Lauren picked up the sandwich and stared down at it briefly. "How did you know I like brie and bacon sandwiches?" she asked in disbelief.

Gillian's eyes sparkled roguishly. "Oh, I just took you for the type."

"Really?" That surprised her. Not even Calum would have been able to guess something like that.

"And I thought you might enjoy this for your afters," Gillian said handing her a large slice of carrot cake.

Lauren's eyes widened. *This is unbelievable.* Maybe she'd got Gillian wrong, she wasn't cocky after all, just very thoughtful. Lauren gave herself a quick word of warning before she got too carried away. *This is not a date. This is a business lunch.*

***

The sound of a grandfather clock ticked loudly in the background as Gillian settled onto her seat, and the women ate in a comfortable silence. Gillian was the first to speak.

"So how long have you been working for your parents?" she asked between mouthfuls of her sandwich.

Lauren dabbed her lips with her napkin and waited until her mouth was empty before speaking. "Oh, about three years now, sort of full-time. I started helping out after school. But after University didn't work out so well, I decided to do this instead."

"What was wrong with Uni?"

"Nothing, except for the going to classes and writing part."

Gillian laughed. "Ah yes, well, that does put a dampener on things."

"It definitely did for me. I loved expanding my knowledge through reading, but that was about all."

"Maybe you should have been a researcher of some kind," she suggested.

"To be honest, I don't think academia in any sense was going to be right for me." A smile tugged at the corner of Lauren's mouth. "So anyway, I had to get a job, and my parents needed the help so here I am."

"What does your husband do if you don't mind me asking?" Gillian said nodding towards the framed photograph of Calum and Scruff on her desk.

"Calum's a junior doctor. He's hoping to go into Paediatric Oncology."

"Really? Wow. What a field. You must be very proud."

"Yes, I am. He works very hard and is really dedicated."

"That is so cool. So you're a doctor's wife. You're

not going to live at the country club in between hot yoga classes, I hope?"

"Um yeah. You definitely don't know me that well. My idea of yoga is bending over to pick up Scruff. And a country club? I'd be kicked out the first day when I asked on a scale of one to ten the level of appropriate snootiness expected."

In the midst of laughter, Gillian said, "That would probably do it."

"So how about you?" Lauren asked.

"What about me?"

"Well, did you always want to be an accountant?"

"No, my ambition was to be a model on the cover of Vogue and travel the world in first class. You know, the whole teenage fantasy thing." She smiled ruefully.

"So what happened?"

"Well, I achieved my dream of being on the cover of Vogue when I was eighteen, but I found out the hard way there are some, shall we say, not very nice people in the business."

"Because of a few arseholes, you gave up a lifestyle us mere mortals could only dream of, for accounting?" Lauren said with an incredulous stare.

Gillian's features darkened. "There was more to it than that, stuff I'd rather forget about," she said tightly, before inhaling and letting out a deep breath. "Besides, I've been happier since I gave it up. I like being my own boss, and I've always had a love affair with maths so it's a good match."

"Fair enough." Lauren smiled and nodded. It was obvious by the hurt in Gillian's eyes that something in her past still had a painful effect on her, so Lauren didn't probe any further. "Has anything stood out with the accounts yet?" she asked, swiftly changing the subject.

"Ahhh the small talk is over I see," Gillian arched an eyebrow and her face suddenly brightened.

Lauren inwardly cringed. She hoped Gillian hadn't mistaken her lack of prying as a show of disinterest. "Well, no, I just meant …" Lauren stammered.

The ringing of Gillian's phone stopped Lauren digging her hole any deeper.

She watched with concern as Gillian's forehead creased with worry and the hand she held the phone with began to tremble.

Chapter Fourteen

"Travis, listen to me very carefully. Stay right where you are and I'll be with you as soon as I can. Do you hear me? Wait there," Gillian spoke with great urgency.

Gillian could hear Travis mumble something incoherent before the line went dead. She snapped her phone shut and scooped up her bag.

"I'm sorry, Lauren; an emergency has come up. I have to go."

"Of course. Is there anything I can do?"

Gillian shook her head. "No, I don't even know what the problem is myself yet." She stood and hurried to the door, then turned around when she reached it. "I'll see you in the morning."

"Yes, of course. I hope everything will be alright."

So did Gillian. As she made her way out onto the street she tried calling Travis several times only to hear the pre-recorded voicemail message: "The mobile number you have called may be switched off."

She hailed an oncoming taxi. "Soho, please," she said as she jumped in the back and slammed the door shut.

She wasn't overly worried about Travis at the moment. She didn't think his emergency would be anything more than a silly argument with Cody. Or something to do with Cody's mum not liking him – though she couldn't imagine that. Everyone loved Travis. The only thing that played on her mind was the fear in his voice. She had never heard him speak that way before. *I hope to God Cody hasn't dumped him.* The taxi soon came to a halt at her destination. Gillian paid the driver and quickly hurried to the bench on Dean Street where Travis said he would be. She knew it well. It was their favourite spot where, in the summer, they'd sit, eat ice cream and watch the world go by.

She caught sight of him from ten yards away. Shoulders hunched; his elbows rested on his thighs. She could tell he was crying by the way his upper body shook. She ran the rest of the distance until she reached him. Resting her hand on his shoulder, she crouched down beside him and buried her face in the crook of his neck.

"I'm here, Travis. I'm here, and it's alright."

He flung his arms around her, gripping her tightly. She felt his body vibrate beneath her fingers.

"Gillian. What am I going to do?"

He turned to face her with tear stained cheeks. She had never seen him look so bad.

"What's happened? Is Cody alright?"

He nodded frantically. "It's me, Gillian. It's me."

"What's you? Tell me so I can help you, please, Travis," she pleaded, a lump forming in her throat.

He wiped his tears away with the back of his hand. "What am I going to do, Gillian?" he asked staring into the distance.

"I'm sure it's not as bad as you think. Whatever it is, we'll get through it. I promise." She smoothed back his chestnut hair and tried to give him a reassuring smile.

Dipping his chin, he turned his head away. "Cody asked me to marry him yesterday," he said as he started to cry again.

Gillian playfully slapped his shoulder. "Jesus Christ, Travis. Are you trying to kill me? I thought there was something wrong." She exhaled a deep breath. "That's fantastic news, I think." Travis had only known Cody for three months and Gillian hadn't even met him yet. But from the way Travis spoke about him, their love for each other had been instantaneous, so who was she to judge? She wholeheartedly believed you could fall in love at first sight.

Gillian frowned when she noticed he was avoiding her gaze. He could be such a drama queen sometimes. She reached up and turned his face to hers. "You didn't turn him down did you? I mean, it was only yesterday you were telling me we only get one shot at life and you were going to grab it with both hands," she teased with a smile.

Travis tilted his head back and closed his eyes. "Gillian … I tested HIV positive!"

Gillian's eyes blinked rapidly. She opened her mouth in an attempt to force comforting words past the lump in her throat, but nothing came out.

"I can't believe this has happened to me."

Gillian pulled him into her arms, kissing the top of his head as he rested his face against her chest. She knew he was waiting to hear her say something, but she was too stunned to even get her thoughts straight.

Travis and HIV? It was an unbelievable scenario. What could she tell him that he didn't already know? That HIV was no longer a death sentence and that if he took his medication he could live to a ripe old age. Instead of acting like a dithering fool, she had to be the pillar of strength he needed.

She cupped his cheeks and held his gaze. "Travis, I love you like you're my own brother. I'm not going to patronise you and say this isn't a biggie. You're healthy and …" She stopped talking. She could hear how futile her words sounded. Travis's world had just crashed around him, and she was giving him useless platitudes.

She wiped the tears from his cheeks. "Shit, Travis. I don't know what to say. Just know that you're not on this journey alone. I'm going to be there with you all the way?"

He shook his head. "I work as an HIV advocate and spend most of my time talking about prevention. How ironic it seems now I've got the virus myself."

He dropped his head and all she could do was sit there and watch him as he silently wept.

Chapter Fifteen

Lauren checked her watch for the tenth time in what seemed like five minutes. *10:00*. Gillian still hadn't shown up for work. She assumed whatever caused her to leave in such a rush the day before was more serious than she had thought. Gillian didn't strike her as the sort of person to shirk her responsibilities at the drop of a hat. No sooner had the thought crossed her mind she heard the chime of the shop door opening. She hoped it was Gillian. It had surprised her how quickly she had come around to seeing her as more of a friend than just a sexual titillation. A friend that she was beginning to care deeply about, despite having known her for only a short amount of time.

Under normal circumstances, it bothered her when Calum didn't return home until the early hours of the morning. But yesterday she'd actually been relieved. Instead of wondering where Calum was she had spent the whole evening worrying about Gillian. She had been tempted to text her and see if she was alright but she didn't know if Gillian would view it as an intrusion.

Lauren hurried to her door and opened it just as Gillian was within a few feet. Her hair was pulled back into a ponytail, and she wore large sunglasses. Lauren's heart sank. *It must have been bad.*

Lauren leaned against the door frame awkwardly. "Morning."

Gillian stopped in front of her, without removing her glasses. "Morning."

Lauren remained quiet for a few seconds. She didn't know Gillian well enough to ask questions of a personal nature but at the same time she couldn't ignore the fact that she seemed upset. "Listen ... umm, you know, if today is not a good day for you, the books can wait."

Gillian reached out and touched Lauren's arm briefly. "Thank you. But it's okay. I'd prefer to be getting on with some work."

Lauren looked down at the spot where Gillian's hand had rested. She could still feel the heat from her touch. "Okay."

"I'll see you later."

Lauren watched as Gillian continued along to her temporary office, before stepping back into her own room and closing the door behind her. She felt helpless. Gillian was obviously in some kind of distress, and there was nothing she could do about it. She spent the next few hours trying to concentrate on her paperwork whilst telling herself that if Gillian wanted to talk she knew where to find her. When midday came and went without Gillian making an appearance, Lauren stood resolutely. Sitting there trying to second guess Gillian's next move was pointless. She grabbed her bag and headed for the coffee shop.

Fifteen minutes later she returned with a coffee, a large hot chocolate, Danishes, freshly baked baguettes and cheeses.

Standing outside Gillian's office, she took a deep breath in preparation, before tapping on the door with her elbow.

Seconds later, the door opened and Gillian stood there, sunglasses-free with puffy red eyes.

Gone was the confident woman that could make her quiver with just a look, in her place was a woman who looked so vulnerable it tore at her heart. "I hope I'm not disturbing you, but I thought …" She nodded her head toward the food. "Unless you're not hungry, that is," she added quickly.

"That's very thoughtful of you," Gillian said glancing at her watch. "I didn't realise it was so late." She opened the door wider to let Lauren enter.

Lauren laid the food and drinks on the table. She eyed Gillian cautiously as she toyed with her baguette.

"Gillian, please tell me to mind my own business if you wish but is everything okay? After yesterday …"

Gillian dropped the baguette onto the table and said, "I heard some upsetting news from an old friend. But it's going to be okay. I'm positive everything will work itself out in the end."

"Oh, I'm glad to hear that." Lauren didn't want to push it any further. It was obvious Gillian didn't want to expand on what she'd said.

Gillian picked up a pile of papers in front of her. "Okay, so back to business. I haven't been through everything yet, but it looks like there are patterns of discrepancies with your shop in Surrey."

Surrey? Her dad had been running that shop for the past few months. "Are you sure it's the one in Surrey?" Lauren asked.

Gillian frowned. "Yes, very."

A weariness permeated Lauren's whole being. So it was true. Her mother had been right with her suspicions. "That's not good," she said more to herself than Gillian.

"Does that mean you have an idea who might be responsible?"

Lauren's eyes half closed as she let out a long sigh. "Maybe." Should she tell her the truth? It took her only a few seconds to know the answer. For some unknown reason, she felt she could trust Gillian.

"I think my dad might be responsible for the missing money."

Gillian's eyebrows contracted slightly. "Your dad? Oh no. Well look. I've only had time to do a very preliminary look," she said quickly. "I haven't reached any final conclusions yet so I don't want you jumping to any either, okay?"

Lauren nodded. "It's going to be hard not to. Damn, why didn't I believe my mum when she told me?"

"Hey, don't beat yourself up about this. I shouldn't have said anything until I was absolutely sure."

"It's okay. I know you're trying to spare my feelings but I'd just rather know." Lauren rubbed the back of her neck. "If you had to guess right now, how much money are we talking about?"

Gillian laced her fingers together in front of her. "I don't like guessing."

Lauren pursed her lips. "I'm not going to hold you to it. It's just I know Mum wouldn't be upset or even concerned about a few quid here and there."

A small sigh escaped Gillian's lips. "Well, I can tell you now it's not a small amount. If I had to give a rough estimate, I'd say close to three hundred thousand."

Lauren jumped up and stared down at her. "Three hundred thousand pounds! Are you serious?"

Gillian held her hands up. "Now, hey, I told you. It's only an estimate. I'm not nearly done going through everything. Chances are I'll find it somewhere else. Honestly, that's how these things usually turn out."

Lauren sat back down. She knew she was pale because she had felt the blood drain from her face. If her father had embezzled that kind of money, it would kill her mother. None of this made any sense. *Oh God, I hope Mum doesn't ask me anything about this when she calls.*

"Okay, I really hope so. My mum said a couple of discrepancies. It never crossed my mind it would be such a large amount. How long do you think it will be before you know for sure?"

"At least a couple of days."

"Okay." Lauren relaxed a little bit. "I certainly feel better having you on board." On one hand, she wanted this cleared up as quickly as possible, on the other, she was afraid of not seeing Gillian again once her job was done.

"I'm glad to hear it, even though I am sorry to be the bearer of bad news." Gillian smiled and casually reached across the desk for Lauren's hand. Her touch sent a sudden jolt through her and she jumped a little, her muscles instantly tightening as she tensed up. She was sure Gillian must have felt it. If she had she didn't seem fazed by Lauren's reaction in the slightest. Instead, Gillian gently squeezed her hand. Lauren felt the tension in her muscles relax. She silently chastised herself for feeling so silly and giddy over having her hand held. She knew it wasn't because she felt embarrassed: No, her out of character response was all down to the woman who was holding it. A million thoughts trampled through her mind. Why was Gillian holding her hand? Was it because she'd felt awful for imparting bad news? Or was it because …? Before the words could form into a question, the front door chimed. Scruff took off ready to defend his castle.

"I'd better see who it is," Lauren said feeling the moment of elation from a few seconds ago evaporate rapidly as Gillian released her hand.

Lauren was shocked to realise that she hadn't felt that kind of connection with anyone in her life before, not even the man she was married to. Reluctantly, she rose to her feet and made her way towards the front of the shop. As she neared she did a double take. There in the doorway, petting Scruff, was Calum holding a bouquet of red roses.

Chapter Sixteen

"Calum?" Lauren said, briefly glancing back towards Gillian's office. "What are you doing here?"

Calum grinned. "What? A husband can't come by and see his wife?"

Lauren willed herself to act normally, as if it was any other day. "Well, of course, silly. I didn't say you couldn't be here." She walked up to him and kissed his cheek. "I'm just surprised that's all. Why aren't you at the hospital?"

"I felt bad for coming home late yesterday, so I thought I'd drop by and surprise my beautiful wife and take her out to lunch." He handed her the roses.

"Oh, Calum, thank you." She took the roses from him and sniffed them. "They're beautiful."

"You're beautiful," he said as he reached out to pull her close.

She struggled against his grip. "Calum, not now," she said quickly. The last thing she wanted was for Gillian to come out and find them in any kind of embrace. She knew she was being silly but somehow she felt as if she was being disloyal to Gillian.

"What's wrong? I thought your parents weren't here."

"They aren't." She cleared her throat in an attempt to rid her voice of any trace of nervousness. "Gillian is here. In the back."

Calum visibly stiffened. "Gillian? Who's Gillian?"

She rubbed her forehead. "Oh crap, I forgot to tell you. Mum thinks someone's fiddling the books, so she hired an accountant."

Deep furrows creased his brow. "How could something like that slip your mind?"

Lauren shrugged. "Can I talk to you about it later? It's getting kind of messy."

"Sure. What about lunch?"

Her fingers twisted her wedding ring. "I'm in the middle of having lunch with Gillian. She bought me lunch yesterday so I thought I'd return the kind gesture," she said truthfully.

"Oh really. I didn't know lunch delivery was a service that accountants provided." His voice had taken on a cooler tone.

She reached out and grabbed is hand, in an attempt to try and defuse the growing tension in the air. Maybe if she introduced her he'd see that she had nothing to hide. "It's a working lunch, Calum. Come and meet her."

They walked to the back, and Lauren made a mental note to go back to the entrance with a mop after the introductions. Damn, Scruff. She was just going to have to buy a decorative mini mop and leave it by the front door.

She led Calum to the office where Gillian was sitting, taking a mouthful of her hot chocolate and reading at the same time. She stood up when she saw them. Lauren began the introductions.

"Gillian, this is Calum, my husband. Calum, this

is Gillian Andrews, our accountant."

"Hi," Calum said, eyeing Gillian closely.

"Hi. Nice to meet you." They exchanged firm handshakes.

"Yeah, you too." He turned abruptly to Lauren. "Do you want me to take the flowers home with me or leave them here?" he asked in a monotone voice.

"What?" She was momentarily taken aback by his blatant rudeness. In all the years she had known him, she had never seen him behave this way before. Lauren looked over at Gillian who appeared to either not have noticed or just didn't care about his attitude.

"No, it's okay. Leave them here. My office could do with a bit of brightening up," she said trying to lighten the mood. "But you can take Scruff back with you if you like, then I can pick us up some dinner on the way home."

"Yeah, okay," he said non-committedly and called for Scruff. Scooping him up, Calum gave a curt nod to Gillian and walked out of the room.

Lauren followed him to the front of the shop. "I'll see you in a few hours?"

"You sure will." The same coolness was in his voice. He gave her a quick peck on the cheek and before she could pull him up on his behaviour, left with Scruff.

As Lauren mopped the front floor again, she couldn't help but wonder why Calum had behaved in the way he had. Had he quietly snuck in to surprise her and seen them holding hands? She didn't think so.

There was no way he could have entered without the door sounding. So what could have sparked him off? She couldn't think of any reason he'd have acted so hostile. She hadn't done anything wrong, not that she could think of anyway. *Well, apart from letting Gillian hold my hand and enjoying every second of it.*

Lauren had never given Calum any reason not to trust her. Even when they had their little break ups here and there before they married, she had never been with anyone else. Not even close. It had always seemed like she and Calum were meant to be together. That was certainly what her parents had wanted. Somehow, it had just become expected that they would get married. By everyone, herself included.

Gillian was in the middle of clearing the table as Lauren walked back into the office.

"How long have you guys been married?" Gillian asked, stopping for a moment.

"Two years, but we dated on and off since we were both sixteen. How about you? Any wedding bells in the near future," she asked, wanting to get off the subject of her rude husband. Besides, she was dying to know Gillian's story.

"Me? You're kidding. I've had enough broken promises and bad shags to last me a lifetime," she joked.

"I'm sure your Prince Charming is out there somewhere for you," Lauren said feeling a tinge of jealously at the thought of Gillian being with anyone but her.

Gillian gave a short laugh. "Princess you mean."

"Sorry?" Lauren asked frowning. *Did I just hear her right?*

"I said my princess is out there somewhere. Not prince. Princes aren't exactly my thing."

"Oh, I see," Lauren said, her heart beating wildly in her chest as the meaning of her words sank in. The memory of Gillian holding her hand replayed vividly in her mind. This new information suddenly put a whole new slant on things. She wasn't just being friendly, Lauren realised with a start. Gillian had been flirting with her – it hadn't been in her imagination. Did that mean Gillian thought she was a lesbian as well? She moved unsteadily backwards towards the door. "I'd better go out front for a bit now. Lucy's out on a delivery and things normally pick up in the afternoon."

"Whatever you say, Lauren. The ball's in your court."

Lauren realised that was a loaded statement. She stumbled out of the door. Was she really that surprised Gillian was gay? She'd given her enough clues? Is that why the atmosphere had been so charged? She needed to be careful – she was fishing in dangerous waters. But why did she feel as if she was the bait?

Chapter Seventeen

Lauren had never understood why some people felt the need to bare their souls to strangers. All she'd done was ask Gillian one simple question about her love life. She hadn't asked her if she was gay. She didn't want to know. It was none of her business. *Damn Gillian for making things even more difficult for me.* Her declaration had only served to muddy the already choppy waters of her life. She was thankful her mother would be back the following day. Even before Gillian had told her she was gay, she'd already decided that she was going to take some time off. She needed to start working on her marriage. Maybe see if a therapist could unravel the mess that was called her mind.

Lauren pulled out her mobile phone as she walked to the tube station.

Hi baby. On my way home. What would you like me to pick up for dinner, or do you want to go out?

She waited for Calum to reply. A few minutes went by and still nothing, so she hopped on the train. Eventually arriving at her stop, and still with no word from Calum, she decided to go to the local Chinese. She was tired and didn't feel like cooking or going out to eat either. Twenty minutes later, she left the Chinese with a hot bag of food.

Reaching the outside of their house, her phone vibrated. *Oh no, please don't want to go out Calum.* Lauren knew if he did, she had better be happy about it, having inadvertently spoilt his lunch. Saying no to dinner would not be the smartest decision.

Hey there. I enjoyed lunch! Maybe we can do it again. Talking shop over food always helps.

Lauren set the bag down and perched on the first step. Before she could stop herself she automatically began to write back a message.

Hey there back! I enjoyed it too. She sent it and waited.

A reply came seconds later.

Maybe we can do it again sometime in a real restaurant?

Lauren held her breath. Is this what she called trying to sort out her marriage? Engaging in texting with a woman she had a schoolgirl crush on? It would break Calum's heart if he even suspected she was playing away – be it physically or emotionally. As much as she wanted to resist, she just couldn't help but feel drawn to Gillian. Being around her was much easier than being with Calum. She had a calming effect on her and Lauren liked that. At times, she felt very small and insignificant around Calum. It seemed like the only time he truly ever wanted to be with her, was when he wanted sex. It was a sad fact but a true one. On the outside, they looked like the picture perfect couple, but scratch the surface and the reality was something altogether different.

Yes, she liked that he was smart and intelligent, but those weren't the things that glued a marriage together. She wanted spontaneity, freedom. In part, things she knew she would never have with Calum. As well as her growing need to explore her sexuality, it was a combination of all of these issues that were responsible for the space that was growing between them.

Her finger hovered over the key. She knew that whatever choice she made, could have the potential to alter her life forever. *Follow your head or your heart?* She tossed the words in her mind. Her heart won.

I would love to! She texted back.

Lauren deleted the messages, then put her phone away as she walked into her dark house. Scruff came tearing down the hall and slid on the hardwood floor and into her ankles.

"Hey, sweetheart!" She bent over and stroked him. "I'm on to you, you little squirt. I'm not picking you up right now." She switched the light on and looked around her feet. Miraculously, the floor was dry.

"Hi, Calum! I'm home," she called out as she made her way to the kitchen. She eyed several empty beer cans strewn across the worktop. That was strange. Calum hardly ever drank during the week. He never knew when he was going to get called in. She set the food on the counter and saw his phone on the kitchen table blinking with messages. She picked it up and saw they were from her, so he had evidently not read them.

"Where's Daddy?" she asked Scruff, who was still bouncing around her feet. She went upstairs to the bedroom. Opening the door to the darkened room, she saw the outline of his body covered in a white sheet. He lay motionless. Calum was out cold. She felt a little annoyed that he hadn't thought to do something nice, like arrange things so they could enjoy their meal at the table. *Like the lunch I had with Gillian.*

But no, it seemed like he was aggravated that his surprise for her didn't work out as he wanted so he came home and drank himself to sleep. She let out a heavy breath. Well, she wasn't going to let him spoil her night. She went back to the kitchen, poured a large glass of wine then took it upstairs with her to the bathroom and ran a bath. Stripping naked, she dropped lavender oil beads into the water and stepped in.

Lauren sunk deeper into the warm water and took a sip of wine. She needed to relax, and there was only one way for her to do that. She closed her eyes and let the fantasy begin.

It's a full moon. A silvery glow fills the bathroom.

I hear a soft knock on the door. "Come in," I whisper.

Gillian pushes the door open, and stands there naked in front of me; slender and toned. The soft moonlight bathes her body. I let my glance glide over her as she loosens her hair from a ponytail, and it spills past her shoulders, across the swell of her breasts. Gillian grins at me and shuts the door quietly behind her. I offer her my glass of wine, and she smiles graciously as she takes it and sits on the edge of the bathtub, swirling her hand lazily in the water.

"I've missed you."

"I've been waiting," I reply in a quivering voice.

Her hand skims the top of the water and makes its way to fondle my breasts. Rubbing and massaging them with sure, confident hands, she grips each of my nipples between her fingers, playfully teasing and twisting them one at a time. I close my eyes as I enjoy the sensation.

"Look over there," she whispers softly, as she points to the massive mirror on the wall opposite the bath. I see the two of us in its golden frame as if in a picture. I can feel my lust and need growing as she reaches down between her thighs and touches herself. I stare at her reflection as she slightly widens her legs and drops her head back as she slowly begins to rub her clit back and forth in one fluid motion.

As she writhes with pleasure, I bury my hand between my legs, inserting my fingers into…

The sound of the door opening jolted Lauren back to the present. Switching the light on, Calum stumbled in. "Sorry, I need to take a leak."

"Holy shit!" Lauren yelled jerking into an upright position, the sudden motion spilling water over the edge of the bath. "You scared the crap out of me."

Calum coughed. "Sorry, needs must."

Yes, he'd definitely had a few before he went to bed. The smell of stale beer emanated from him as he staggered to the toilet and raised the lid. Lauren looked down mournfully at herself in the mirror. The fantasy was over. She was alone, the water was getting cold, and she was staring at the arse of her semi-drunk husband pissing into the toilet. The mood was definitely lost.

Instead of leaving when he'd finished, he closed

the lid and wearily sat down.

"What's the matter?" she asked a little impatiently. She wanted him to go back to bed so she could try and recapture the last part of her fantasy.

"We need to talk," he said scraping his hand over his chin.

She took a sip of her wine. "Well talk then. I'm listening."

"I can't do this any more, Lauren." He cast his eyes downwards.

She snapped her head towards him. "Do what?"

She could see the melancholy look in his eyes.

"Marriage, medicine, living here … it's not what I want. I'm sorry."

Lauren's eyes widened. "Calum, I think that beer has rotted your brain." She heard the panic in her voice.

A faint smile played on his lips. "If it has I highly recommend it. My head is the clearest it's been in years. I've just never had the guts to say what I really think before today."

She rose to her feet and with a trembling hand, reached for the towel and wrapped it around her body.

She watched as Calum left the bathroom without saying another word. Stepping out of the bath onto the cold tiled floor, she wondered for a moment if he'd been sleepwalking. *He'd had enough? Join the bloody club.* Whatever was going on in his head would have to wait until tomorrow to be addressed. Leaving the bathroom, she looked around for Scruff and couldn't see him anywhere. Calum had left the door to the bedroom ajar, so she tiptoed in and felt the little lump under the covers on her side of the bed. Smiling, she slid into bed next to a snoring Calum. She would have to force herself to get up earlier tomorrow, so set the alarm on her phone for 6:00. It was obviously time for them to have "the talk" she had been trying so desperately to avoid.

When she awoke the next morning, the space beside her was empty – Calum had gone. On his pillow, lay a piece of paper.

She picked it up, her heart thumping in the process. Tears blurred her vision as she read the four words written on it – I need to breathe.

Chapter Eighteen

Storm clouds churned, and a clap of thunder rattled the glass window pane. Gillian watched over Travis as he slept through the earth shattering noise, curled up in a foetal position on her bed. The sound of his soft breathing filled the room. To Gillian, he looked so childlike and defenceless that her heart ached. She checked her watch once more and felt a pang of guilt. She didn't want to go to work and leave Travis alone again, but he had insisted she carry on with her life as if he had never told her his news. But how could she? They had been through everything together, but this was one thing she couldn't fix. He uncurled his body, rolled abruptly onto his back and opened one eye.

"If you stare at me one second longer you're going to burn a hole through me." His voice was hoarse.

"I'm sorry." She sat on the bed beside him and rested her hand on his shoulder.

"I'd rather stay here with you than go into work."

"What's that going to solve? Like I said last night, I've got to be proactive. Time isn't on my side any more."

Gillian flinched. "Travis, I don't want to hear you talk like that, do you hear me?" she said, her eyes welling up with tears. She knew Travis always dealt with his stresses with humour and normally she couldn't fault him on this. She couldn't count the times he had brought her down from the edge with his fun-loving ways. But those situations hadn't been as dire as this one.

Travis pushed himself up into a sitting position. "Gill." He swooped her up into his arms and gave her a squeeze. "I'm sorry. That joke was in bad taste."

"Yes, it was," she said extracting herself from his embrace, and playfully slapping his shoulder.

"You know, having HIV doesn't stop me from being an insensitive dick. Would you prefer it if I'd had some kind of epiphany and turned into a saint?"

Gillian groaned. "No, Never! I'll take your inappropriate jokes any time of the day."

"Well, good because it's not going to happen." He lifted her head up. "Now listen to me; I've spent two days wallowing in self-pity–"

Gillian drew back. "–I'd hardly say it was self-pity. You've just found out some pretty devastating news."

"Yes, I have, but crying isn't going to fix it. I've got the virus, and there's nothing I can do about it. Moping around all day isn't going to make it magically go away."

"But–"

He held his hand up to silence her. "No buts, Gillian. These are the cards I've been dealt, and I want to be in control of how they play out. I'm not going to beat myself up about it because it's done; I can't change it. I'm still Travis – who just happens to have HIV," he said matter-of-factly. "Do you know the first thing I say to my clients when they've just been diagnosed? Don't let the virus define you. And I'm going to follow my own advice. So first things first." He edged her off of the bed and shooed her away with a wave of his hand. "You're going to get ready for work, make yourself look all fab and gorgeous and put my problems as far out of your mind as possible."

"And what are you going to do?"

Travis' mobile phone began to vibrate on the bedside table. He gave it a cursory glance and picked it up. "I'm going to face up to my new world without fear," he said pressing the accept button on his phone. "Cody, I'm sorry, don't be angry …" he began in a soothing voice.

But it was to no avail – Gillian could still hear Cody's voice bellowing from the other end of the line. She knew he'd be angry that Travis had been avoiding his calls while he had been holed up in her apartment. She had tried to talk Travis into letting him know that he was safe and that he was with her, but he couldn't bear the thought of hearing his voice at that time. She grabbed her hair band from the dresser, tied her hair into a ponytail and headed to the bathroom to give Travis some privacy. She hoped that once Travis told Cody the truth he'd stand by him and support him. She knew it would be a tough decision to make seeing as they had only known each other for such a short time, but wasn't that what love was all about, tough choices?

Stripping naked, she sighed as she stepped into

the spacious steam shower. She was pleased that Travis was feeling in a more positive mood this morning. He was right with his way of thinking, but that was Travis all over. You could knock him down, time and time again, but it would take a mighty force to stop him getting back up again.

Minutes later she wrapped a large fluffy towel around her body, before walking back to her bedroom to find Travis staring out of the large window that looked down onto the communal garden.

"You know I never realised how beautiful oak trees are until today," he said as she entered the room. "It's a shame it takes a life-threatening disease to make you wake up and smell the coffee."

Her stomach coiled with fear. "How did the talk go with Cody?"

He glanced over at her with a frown. "I'm catching up with him later. He's got an important meeting this morning. No point in spoiling his day before it's even started."

She hated the thought of leaving him alone for even a second despite his act of bravado. She couldn't even begin to imagine how he felt and that's what made the situation even harder. She would have preferred it if he had screamed and yelled about how unfair life was, rather than the way he had quietly accepted his fate as if it were somehow pre-destined. She opened the wardrobe door and let her towel slip to the floor.

"Travis, are you sure you don't want me to stay

here with you?" she asked on the verge of tears again as she put on her bra and underwear.

Travis kept his eyes trained out of the window. "Absolutely, sweetie. Wear something breathtakingly revealing and knock the socks off this woman."

Gillian laughed. "If you saw how hot her husband was you'd know that would be near enough impossible." She opted for a pair of black skinny jeans and a black vest, before deciding the colours were too morbid and quickly changing into blue jeans and a white shirt.

"Looks have nothing to do with anything dear. It's all about what's in the heart."

"Well, if her heart wasn't already taken I'd have to agree," she said walking over to where he stood. "But seeing as it is, I'm going to have to settle for friendship."

"And can you handle that?"

Gillian shrugged. "It's not a question of if I can handle it; sadly it's just a fact."

Chapter Nineteen

Time to get up. Lauren didn't bother looking at the time, she knew without being told that she'd been lying in bed for more than two hours due to daylight emerging from the dark morning sky. During that period, she'd called Calum at least a hundred times only to be met with his pre-recorded voicemail message. On several occasions, she'd been tempted to call his parents but decided she'd rather drown in her own misery than give them the satisfaction of knowing there was discord in their marriage.

She had wrestled with every imaginable scenario that could have caused Calum to suddenly up and leave. Was it work related? Was it her fault? Had she made herself so emotionally unavailable that she had missed the signs that Calum was unhappy? In the end, she'd given up trying to figure it out. There was no point – she knew the answer could only come from the man himself. Calum would have to resurface sooner or later and then they could figure out a way to move forward.

She pulled a disgruntled Scruff out of the covers and took him downstairs with her, where he soon settled happily under the blanket on the sofa. The living room had never looked so tidy. The desk that was normally weighed down with Calum's medical books was bare, bar a thin layer of dust. Clothes, trainers, gym bag – things that were once permanent fixtures – all gone.

Lauren settled next to Scruff and put the TV on. She flipped through the channels and unless she wanted to buy a "Real Faux Diamond" necklace that was available now for the next seven minutes at the astonishingly low price of just four hundred pounds, or start the new guaranteed fat blast pill regime, there was nothing of interest to watch.

Maybe I should do a Calum special and get drunk. Yeah, that will solve all my problems. Except she had to go and open the shop. Her parents wouldn't be back until lunchtime. *Lunchtime? Sweet bliss.* Was it only yesterday that she didn't have a care in the world except for daydreaming about Gillian? *Why is she still crowding my mind when I should be thinking of ways to save my marriage?* She dreaded the thought of having to tell her mum, especially when she'd be breaking the news to her today about the missing money. *Hi, Mum, welcome back. Just to let you know you were right about Dad, he's stolen about three hundred thousand pounds and guess what? My mind's been so wrapped up with that sexy accountant you hired, I didn't realise my husband was so miserable he was on the verge of leaving. Other than that, it's business as usual.* Yeah, right. That could cause her mum to have a heart attack on the spot. *Could I be charged with something like involuntary manslaughter?*

Despite her sour mood, Lauren laughed at the idea. Scruff jerked his head and growled. "Okay, okay. I'm sorry." Apparently she wasn't allowed to laugh under such sombre circumstances. *Even my dog has a say on my behaviour. Jesus.*

"The world doesn't stop spinning because he's left, Scruff," she said, bending over to kiss his head. "And I need a strong cup of coffee if I'm ever going to get to work."

In the kitchen, she poured herself a cup and was nursing her drink when she glanced down and saw Scruff sitting patiently by the door. Lauren groaned. The last thing she wanted was to take him out for his morning pee. Why he couldn't go in the back garden like any other normal dog she didn't know. But ever since they'd had him he would pee anywhere but their garden.

"Okay then, let's go." She went into the bathroom and pulled her hair up into a ponytail, then grabbed her jacket off the clothes hook by the door. She was still in her flannel jammies, but she didn't care. That's how it was in London these days. People in their jammies and slippers, out with their dogs early in the morning and no one batted an eyelid. She picked him up, and he licked the side of her face.

"Thanks, Scruff. At least you still love me," she said as she opened the front door. The brisk air, when it hit her, felt like walking into a freezer, and not for the first time did she wish Scruff could use the house toilet. Every time she thought about it, she pictured him jumping up and falling right into the toilet bowl. That would be worse than or at least as bad as these early morning pee patrols.

The wind blew hard against her cheeks, and little

droplets of rain fell on the floor.

"Hurry up, Scruff. It's freezing." She watched him walk, circle and sniff until he found the spot that smelt right to pee in, and then did his thing. A few steps and circles later, he got the rest of his business done, and Lauren bagged it and tossed it in the bin.

Minutes later they were back in the warmth of their house, and she realised sadly she'd have to go back into the freezing cold in a short while. What she really wanted to do was go to sleep then wake up and find this had all been a nightmare. Everything – her fantasies, the theft from the business and Calum leaving. But when she went upstairs and opened the wardrobe door, the stark reality of the situation hit her like a tonne of bricks. Calum's space was empty. She must have been in a hell of a deep sleep that he'd managed to pack all his belongings without waking her. Lauren checked her phone again. She wanted to believe that Calum had texted or called when she'd been out walking Scruff, but he hadn't. She threw her phone down on the bed in disgust. She felt hurt and angry. She was sure he must have picked up her numerous messages by now, but he still didn't have the decency to reply. *Well, sod him; let him play his silly games.* She decided not to contact him again and instead play him at his own game and see how he liked it.

Lauren quickly selected her clothes for work and slammed the wardrobe door shut. Maybe work was the best place for her to be, so his absence didn't make her feel like she'd been kicked in the gut every time she looked around their home and realised he might not ever be coming back.

***

Lauren barely had time to remove her jacket and put the heater on in her chilly office when there was a gentle tap on the door. She looked up as Gillian appeared in the doorway holding a bunch of folders.

"Am I interrupting anything? I think I've found out how the money's been taken."

"Wow, already. Please come in."

"I told you I liked numbers," Gillian said, as she walked further into the room and closed the door behind her.

Scruff ran up to her, and she bent over to greet him. "Awww hello, Scruff." She ruffled the top of his head. "Have you come to pee on my boot?"

Lauren laughed. Seeing Gillian made her realise she'd made the right decision in going to work and not sitting at home feeling sorry for herself.

"You look distracted. Everything okay?" Gillian asked, looking over at her.

Lauren honestly didn't know how to respond. Calum had left her but being in the room with Gillian at that moment in time she couldn't have cared less. Did that make her a bad person? Perhaps Calum's parents had been right – she wasn't the right woman for him. Maybe he had just realised this for himself, and that's why he had taken off so suddenly.

"What? Oh, yes. I was just thinking about some

deliveries that are due this morning."

"In that case I won't keep you long."

"No, please stay as long as you like. I could do with some company." She hoped Gillian couldn't hear the desperation in her voice.

Gillian threw a surprised look at her. "Well, you sure know how to brighten up a girl's morning."

Lauren pulled a face. "I'm glad I do something for someone," she said wearily.

"Oh?" Gillian looked at her enquiringly.

Lauren gave a wave of her hand. "It's nothing. Ignore me. Sometimes I feel as old as these antiques," she said picking up an old watch and turning it over in her hand.

"Do you enjoy working here?" Gillian sat down and laid the folders on the desk.

Lauren cocked her head. "Do you mean with the antiques or for my parents?"

"Both, I guess." Gillian laughed.

Lauren dropped into her chair and leaned back. She couldn't figure out why she liked talking with Gillian so much. It was like having a sister to confide in. Maybe that was why she decided to avoid giving her the usual spiel she normally spat out when people asked her the same question.

"To be honest, no. No, I don't," she stated slowly. "This is not how I imagined my life to be at this age."

Gillian raised an eyebrow. "I admire your honesty. I don't know many people that will admit that life isn't going in the direction they wanted it to."

"I wouldn't normally but …"

"But?"

Biting her lip, she looked away. "But I can talk to you. I don't feel as if you'll judge me, no matter what I say."

"Well, you're a good judge of character because I won't."

"I know and that's what I like about you. And if you must know, the reason I hate working here is because," she paused, "I just feel as if I'm watching life pass me by and I don't have any say in it."

"What would you rather be doing?"

"That's just it. I don't know." She searched her mind for a plausible explanation. "I'm not one of these ambitious people with milestones set in place to achieve something by a certain age or by a certain time. I like to read, spend time with Scruff, and watch movies. It might be boring, and I might seem dim for not wanting to be the CEO of an FTSE one hundred company or go skydiving over Niagara Falls. I don't want to be judged for just wanting to be happy. And more than anything, I want someone to be happy with."

"So I take it you're not happy with your husband?" Gillian asked.

Lauren stirred uneasily in her chair. She had let the last bit slip out before she'd even realised she'd said it. But she didn't care. It felt liberating to tell the truth.

"No, not most of the time. He lives to work, and

that seems to be his main priority. I don't think I'm enough for him."

Gillian's expression grew still and serious. "I can't ever imagine you not being enough for anyone."

Lauren gave her a bleak, tight-lipped smile. "You think so?"

She nodded her head decisively. "Yes, I do."

Lauren's voice broke miserably. "Then maybe you can explain, why, if I'm enough, my husband walked out of our marriage yesterday?"

Gillian's hand flew to her mouth. "Oh my God, Lauren … I didn't … I'm sorry."

Lauren smoothed back her hair. "It's okay, really," she said feeling the tears well in her eyes.

"No, it's not. You must be devastated. I thought something was up when he dropped by yesterday."

Wow. She doesn't miss anything. Maybe that's an accountant thing, scrutinise all the details.

"I thought you hadn't noticed?"

"It would have been hard not to. The atmosphere was a bit fraught, to say the least. Had you been arguing or something?"

The muscles in her throat constricted as a tear slipped from her eye. "Nope. That's the thing; his leaving just came out the blue. Totally unexpected." She rubbed the back of her neck. "It's most probably a work thing and he's gone off to lick his wounds somewhere."

Gillian nodded in agreement as she half stood and leaned across the desk to wipe the tear from

Lauren's cheek. "I can imagine. It must be very stressful being surrounded by sick people every day," she said sitting back down.

Lauren dropped her lashes to hide the hurt in her eyes. "Anyway, enough of my woes. I'm sure you've got enough of your own problems without me adding to them," she said, trying her hardest to sound sweetness and light.

"I'm here whenever you want to talk. Any time at all," she replied with a tenderness in her voice that made Lauren feel even worse.

Lauren forced a smile. "Thanks. I'm sure I'll figure my life out sometime."

"I hope you do. I really do."

Lauren's heart swelled. She knew she shouldn't be having feelings like this for Gillian or anyone else for that matter. Especially at a time like this when her marriage was on the brink. But with this woman she couldn't help it. Gillian had awoken some part of her that she never even knew existed. What would Calum think if he knew she had been yearning for a woman's touch way before she had even met him? That it wasn't until she had met Gillian that her unspoken need had been fully ignited.

Guilt consumed her as Gillian picked up the files from the desk and flicked through them. Why wasn't she out there looking for Calum? She was his wife for Pete's sake. She had taken vows and made promises. For better, for worse, till death do us part. Instead, she was sat rooted to her chair, wishing she could be with

Gillian for an eternity.

"So," she said clasping her hands together on the desk. "Tell me what you've found."

Gillian cleared her throat. "Ok, well. I've gone through all the invoices for the last year. I've checked them and re-checked them, and I'm sorry, Lauren, but my suspicions were right. The money is definitely missing from the Surrey premises."

Two knock backs in one morning – weren't things meant to happen in threes? Where would the next blow come from?

"There's a supplier," Gillian said laying the papers in the middle of the desk so Lauren could see them, "Stratworth Antiques, who have been paid large amounts of money. I cannot find any record of the items purchased being sold, and they are not on the stock list. There's also no listing for the business at Companies House and no other trace of them anywhere."

Lauren's mouth dropped open. Her emotions quickly changed from upset to anger.

"So what you are saying is that my dad has set up a dummy company to embezzle money to?"

"I'm afraid so. That's not all either. I've discovered that another bank account in the company's name has been set up, and I believe deposits that were due to be paid in to Tate's antiques, have actually been paid to this other account. No doubt this is what initially alerted your accountant."

Lauren ran her fingers through her hair. "It just gets worse. Can you tell when this started?"

"Yes, June last year. Just after the last accounts were filed. The person knew that would give them time," Gillian said, tapping a date she had circled in red ink.

"And it's three hundred thousand?"

Gillian reached for another sheet of paper. "Well, slightly over. In total three hundred and twelve thousand pounds."

Lauren opened her mouth and promptly snapped it shut. She was speechless. Lauren felt like someone had whacked her on the head with a baseball bat. She felt dizzy as the truth dawned on her. There was no doubt in her mind whatsoever now that it was her father. Who else had the authority to purchase stock and set up bank accounts? None of it made any sense. Did it really cost that much to keep a mistress? The thought of having to tell her mother made her feel sick to the stomach.

Lauren made a moue of disappointment. "Are you absolutely sure? I mean, well, yes I'm sure you are but is there any way something has been overlooked?"

Gillian shook her head sadly. "No. From the paperwork I have, this is my conclusion. The money I've mentioned is unaccounted for."

Lauren sighed. "This is going to kill my mum," she mumbled. "Two divorces in the same month, great."

"I'm sure it's not going to come to that. If your father is responsible, he might have a perfectly legitimate explanation. It doesn't necessarily have to be something bad. It's just human nature to jump to that conclusion. Maybe, I don't know, he wanted to buy your mum something nice."

Lauren sucked in her bottom lip before replying. "For over three hundred grand!?"

Gillian laughed nervously. "Okay, well maybe not a surprise. Look, you know your father better than anybody, what do you think he spent it on?"

"That's where you're wrong, Gillian. I don't think I do know him. I don't think I know anyone any more."

"I'm sorry. I wish I could make this easier for you."

Lauren's eyes roamed along Gillian's arms. She had a wild urge to throw herself into them. She lifted her gaze, and as their eyes met, she thought she saw something in Gillian's, some flicker of … Oh, she didn't know. Probably wishful thinking. *Just because she's a lesbian don't mistake her kindness for her having the hots for you.*

The sound of the front door opening broke the moment. "That's probably a customer. I think it's best I break the news to my mum," Lauren said flatly as she rose to her feet and walked to the door. Gillian followed, stopping inches away from her.

"I hope we can remain friends, Lauren." She held out her hand and enclosed Lauren's within it.

"Me too."

"And I hope to see Scruff again as well, even if it's to let him pee on me."

Lauren laughed. Even with the crappiness of this day, she loved that Gillian could still make her laugh. She reached down for the handle and opened the door. "I'm sorry. I don't know how this works. Do I pay you now or …?"

"What? Oh no. Don't worry about it. I'll get my time sheets together and go over them with your mum. There's no rush. I've got pot noodles to last me through next week," she joked.

"Alright. Thank you." Lauren smiled. "It's been a pleasure. I mean, not really, but … well, you know what I mean."

"For me too," Gillian said taking a step towards her.

They were standing so close that Lauren could feel the heat from Gillian's body.

"I know we haven't met under the best of circumstances, but …" Gillian's words trailed off as she slowly reached up and brushed Lauren's hair away from her face.

For a split second, Lauren thought Gillian was going to kiss her. If she had, she would have welcomed it in a flash. She wanted to close her eyes, and have Gillian's lips claim her own. To pull her tight against her and feel the softness of her body mould into hers.

Gillian had the power to make her forget all that was wrong in her world right now. For just a moment, everything would be right. But then, she thought, realistically, everything would soon be all wrong again. Jumping from the frying pan into the fire wasn't going to solve anything.

"I hate goodbyes," Lauren said, drawing back a little, feeling the need to put some distance between them.

"It doesn't have to be forever. You know I'm only a phone call away if you ever need me … for anything?" she said softly.

Lauren dropped her eyes to the ground. "Why does everything good have to be so complicated?" she said out loud without thinking. She couldn't bear the thought of not seeing Gillian again.

Gillian's hand reached under her chin, and she raised Lauren's eyes back to hers.

"I know we can be nothing but friends and I'm alright with that. I just wanted you to know in case you think I want something you can't give me."

"I …" Lauren said softly. She struggled to find a way to tell her that she wanted the same and more. That she knew it was crazy but she had fallen for her, lock, stock and barrel. But what good would it do? What did she have to offer Gillian? Would the whole of her heart be enough? She heard her phone chirp, and looked towards it on the desk, but remained where she stood.

Gillian tilted her head to the side. "Do you think you should answer it?" Her voice was like a caress against her skin.

Lauren could feel her face heating up underneath her intense gaze. "No. It can wait." She was relieved when the phone went silent and then opened her mouth to speak. It was now or never. "Gillian …" she paused open-mouthed. The phone started to ring again "Damn!"

Gillian nodded towards the phone. "It might be important."

"But …"

"It's okay." She leaned forward, pressed her face gently against Lauren's cheek and whispered in her ear. "You don't have to say anything. I know."

Without another word, she turned and walked away.

Even she knows any chance of being together is impossible. With her heart in her mouth, Lauren watched Gillian retreat down the corridor until she disappeared from view. She bowed her head as she crossed the floor to her desk. Picking up her phone, she glanced down at the screen and took a deep breath before answering it.

"Calum, what the hell are you playing at?" she asked ferociously. Even as she spoke she was aware of being angrier at her predicament rather than him.

"We need to talk. Meet me at my mum's tonight at six."

"Why …?"

The line went dead, and Lauren was drawn back into her world of drama.

Chapter Twenty

"So let me get this right, that snivelling little bastard has taken me for three hundred thousand pounds?" Jean's high-pitched voice bounced off the walls, as she paced the floor in her office like a hungry lion.

Lauren didn't think this was the best time to tell her it was actually £312,000, but hey, what was a few thousand here or there. "Shhh Mum, everyone will hear you."

"And I should care why exactly?" She narrowed her eyes. "Did your father care when he was stealing money from the company that's kept a roof over his head all these years?" Her voice rose a little louder. "Did he hell! I'll cut his tiny pair of balls off when I get hold of him."

Lauren pressed her lips together in a slight grimace. "Er hello, too much information there." She heaved a sigh. "Okay, I can understand why you're angry, so am I, but what's important now is the next step. What are you going to do to get the money back?"

Jean waved her hand dismissively. "I'm going to call the police, what else?"

"Mum, at least speak to him first. There might be a reasonable explanation," she said as the image of the package that had been delivered for her father came into her mind. *Maybe he'll sweet talk Mum tonight and all will be forgiven.* While the thought was nice, she didn't think it was a very realistic one. Her mother had every right to be as angry as she was. This was the one time she wouldn't be supporting her father. How could she?

Jean wrung her hands together in frustration. "Lauren, I don't care what excuse he comes up with. Unless it was to pay for life saving surgery, nothing can excuse what he's done."

"Oh, come on, Mum," Lauren pleaded desperately. "At least hold off calling the police until you've spoken to him. Then you can reassess the situation. Whatever you decide, I promise I will support your decision."

Jean raised her eyebrows questioningly. "What does Calum think of all this?"

"Um, he doesn't know it was Dad," she said, dropping her gaze to the ground. She didn't know why she'd been reluctant to tell Calum. Shame? Embarrassment? Most probably both. She would actually consider disappearing in the middle of the night if his parents caught a whiff of this scandal. She'd never live it down.

"Ha!" Jean barked. "You're too ashamed to tell him aren't you? I don't blame you. Poor man's got the world on his shoulders without our family dramas heaped on top."

Lauren fought to keep her tone strong. The last thing she wanted to do was break down in front of her mother. Especially when she was in one of her unsympathetic moods. No doubt she'd put all the blame on her for being such a crap inattentive wife.

"Calum left me last night."

"I don't know how I'm going to look your father in the–" Jean stopped abruptly. "What did you just say?"

"I said, Calum left me last night," she replied a little more forcefully.

Jean looked back at her with an incredulous stare. "What do you mean left you? Married men don't just up and leave their wives."

Lauren rubbed her hand over her face and blew out a breath. "Well mine does, and he has," she said in defeat.

"I don't understand," Jean mumbled as she slowly sat down on the chair at her desk. "You've both got the world at your feet."

"Obviously the world isn't enough for him, maybe he wants the universe as well."

Jean looked as if all the air had been sucked out of her. Maybe it hadn't been such a good idea to tell her about Calum on the back of the shocking news about the missing money. She felt sorrier for her mum than she did for herself.

"I take it he's gone back to his mum's?"

"It would appear so. I'm meeting him there tonight. He said he wanted to talk."

"About?" she said wearily.

Lauren shrugged her shoulders. "Dunno. He didn't say."

Jean avoided looking up at her and instead began to tidy her imaginary messy desk. "Look Lauren, tell me to mind my own business but …"

Lauren's voice quivered, and tears streaked down her pale cheeks. "Don't you dare try and lay the blame for this on me. Don't you dare!" She roughly wiped away the tears with her fist. "I'm not the one who walked out of this marriage; he did!"

Jean stood and quickly walked around her desk, then pulled Lauren into her arms.

"Shhh come on, sweetheart," she said patting her back. "If you had given me a second to speak I would have told you not to go round there begging for crumbs from him."

Lauren's anger simmered. Her mother's tone was actually maternal which both surprised and comforted her. It had been a long while since her mother had given her any comfort in a moment of crisis. Normally she'd just lay the blame at her feet regardless of who was right – especially when it came to Calum. Sometimes Lauren believed she would rather have had him as a son instead of her.

Jean leaned back and wiped away Lauren's smudged mascara with her thumb.

"Calum's lucky to have found someone like you, and if he can't appreciate you I'm sure there'll be plenty of men who can." Jean straightened Lauren's collar. "Come on now, where's that tough spirit of yours?"

Lauren managed a weak smile.

Jean squeezed her cheek. "That's my girl. If there's one thing I've tried to instil in you growing up, it's that you don't need anybody. You can fare well enough on your own!"

For the first time in years, her mother had let her defences down, and Lauren felt that mother and daughter bond she had seen in so many of her friends' families. Seizing the moment to explore these new uncharted waters, she said, "I can't understand why he never spoke to me about being unhappy."

Jean snorted. "If he's anything like your father, you'll never know."

"If that's the case, our marriage will be well and truly over," she said with only a slight hesitation. It would feel strange to be single and on the meat market, as her friends so eloquently called being on the dating scene. It was something she'd never considered before. When she had taken her vows, as far as she was concerned, they were forever.

They were both startled as they heard the door handle turn. "That's your dad," Jean whispered quickly. "Not a word. I'll deal with this in my own way."

Lauren nodded.

"Now wipe those tears away and stand up straight. Don't give anyone the power to break you."

Ken entered the room smiling. "Lauren, I just came from your office. I wondered where you were."

"Hi, Dad," she said as he walked over and hugged her.

When she stiffened in his arms, he said, "Are you okay? You look upset."

She took a step back and said the first thing that

came to mind. "Um, hay fever, I think."

Ken looked at her questioningly. "At this time of year?"

"Yeah, I know, crazy isn't it?"

He patted her shoulder. "Okay, well let me know if you need anything from the chemist." He rubbed his hands together. "Now, when are you and Calum going to come around for dinner? It's been ages since we've seen you both. How about tonight?"

"Lauren's busy tonight," Jean interjected. "And so are we."

Ken looked at her. "We are?"

"Yes, Ken, we are. Very, very busy," she said, her tone full of intent.

Lauren looked from her mother to her father. He looked stricken. Had he figured out that her mum was on to him? Her heart ached for him as he stood there looking like a little boy waiting for his punishment to be dished out. As Lauren saw her mother's mouth open, she threw him a lifeline she knew he didn't deserve. But she didn't want to be there when the truth came out.

"Dad, I forgot to say, a package arrived for you. It's in my office. Do you want to come and get it now?"

Ken looked at Jean, who in turn looked at Lauren with disappointment then without a word, strode out of the room.

"You'll be in trouble for that," Ken warned her as they made their way to her office.

"I'll get her some flowers later and take her out for lunch." She walked over to the window ledge and grabbed his package. "Someone's in for a nice surprise tonight." As Lauren turned to give it to him, she felt her heart turn over as she looked into the eyes of a guilty man.

"You know what's in that package, don't you?" he asked meekly.

Lauren nodded, not trusting herself to speak.

Ken scraped his hand over his face. "It's a surprise for your mother."

"Don't lie to me, Dad. On top of everything else, please don't lie."

He took a step forward. "Listen, Lauren, it's not what you think."

Lauren widened her eyes. "What do I think, Dad?"

He let out a long sigh as he ran his fingers through his hair. "That it's for someone else."

"And is it?"

His face crumpled. "No ... I ..."

Before he could say another word she threw the package at him, landing it squarely against his chest. "Oh my God, Dad. How could you do this to Mum? How could you?" she spat out angrily.

"Please, Lauren, let me explain." Ken held out his hands to her.

Lauren recoiled from his touch. She must have been out of her mind to think her dad was a decent man. It seemed like everyone in her world was hiding some kind of secret for one reason or another.

"Don't bother with your lies. Mum was right about you. I hope you get all you deserve and more," she screamed at the top of her lungs as she fled the room choking back the tears.

Damn her for being so trusting. When was she going to learn not to take everything she was told at face value? She knew it was time to remove her rose tinted glasses. Nobody was perfect. Not even her dad. Surely she only had to look at her own life to see how easy it was to hide things from the people you claimed to love.

Chapter Twenty-One

Gillian was starting to think that anyone who came into contact with her was cursed. First Travis, now Lauren breaking up with her husband. As much as she liked her, she didn't want her life to fall apart at the seams. Maybe she should wear a warning sign. *Get to know me at your peril.*

For the first time in ages, she was at a loss what to do. After she'd left Lauren's shop that morning, she had been feeling a kind of separation anxiety; having taken to Lauren in a way she'd never experienced with anyone before. *And this is why you should be a bit more cautious before letting unavailable women into your life.*

Gillian entered the bar and ordered her first drink of the day, a large glass of red wine. There were an endless number of people she could have called to join her, but she hadn't wanted any company. Today was the fifth anniversary. An anniversary for which she was lucky to still be alive.

"Another, Gill?"

Gillian looked down at her empty glass. "Yes, please, Robin. A brandy this time," she said to the bartender. She'd been going to Robin's long enough to be on first name terms with the owner. It was the sort of place women went to forget their troubles and maybe pick up new ones like she had with Stella. Gillian had been young and impressionable when she'd met Stella, the owner of Lambert's model agency who she was contracted to. Being ten years older than herself, Stella knew exactly how to manipulate her, and she had remained under her spell for years.

Stella had lied when she'd told her she was single. Gillian had found out she was in fact married with two children. She had lied again when she said she loved her more than anything in the world. She had lied when she said she couldn't leave her husband because he was suicidal and would kill himself if she did. She didn't lie when she said she would kill Gillian if she ever tried to leave her. Though faded, her skin still bore the sixteen scars the knife had made when she dared to say enough was enough; five years ago today she had been knocking on death's door. *Stella, what a ride!*

"Ain't seen you in here in a long time. What brings you back today?" Robin said, placing a glass of brandy in front of her.

"It's just one of those days. Just one of those days." She knocked back her drink and slid her empty glass towards her. "Another, please."

"Sure thing," Robin said refilling her glass.

Gillian's phone started to ring, and she considered ignoring it before noticing it was Travis. She answered while taking a sip of her drink.

"I'm so sorry, babe," he said his voice full of regret.

"Why? What's happened?"

"I've been so wrapped up in my own thoughts I'd forgotten it's slasher day today."

The crude name was an attempt to take the sting out of the memory.

"Don't be silly, Travis. You've got more important things to worry about than my past."

"I should be with you."

"No, you should be where you are, sorting your life out with your partner. He's so lucky to have you, Travis."

"That remains to be seen. Oh, he's here now. Listen, honey, don't deny it but I know you're on the booze. Don't overdo it and please, if it gets too much for you call me, no matter how late it is. Love you. Kiss, kiss."

"Love you too."

Gillian smiled and disconnected the call. She prayed his conversation with Cody would go well. If Cody rejected him now, she didn't know how she would pick up the pieces.

Thinking about rejection, she shook her head. How could Calum have walked out on Lauren? Couldn't he see how lucky he was to have a woman like her? It had taken everything in her power not to kiss Lauren before she'd left earlier. She had been shaken by the intensity of emotion she had felt when saying goodbye. It was as if she was leaving a part of herself behind.

She knocked back her drink and signalled for another one. It had only been a few hours since leaving Lauren's office, but she was already missing her like she'd just lost the love of her life.

Chapter Twenty-Two

Lauren felt dwarfed by the sprawling townhouse she stared at in the distance. To say it was a mansion was an understatement. The building seemed to go on forever, length and height wise. After waiting for over ten minutes, the metal gates finally opened, and Lauren began the long walk up the gravel path towards the front door. No doubt Calum's mother had been watching her on the security camera, waiting to see if she'd turn around and go home. There was no way she was going to give her that satisfaction. She was here to see Calum and find out what the hell was going on. One way or another she wanted to know where she stood.

Lauren plastered a fake smile on her face as the door opened, and Calum's mum stood in the doorway.

"Good evening, Mrs. Parker."

"Lauren," she said coolly, as she eyed her from head to toe as if she'd just scraped her off the bottom of her shoe. "You know I don't like being called Missus, it ages me dreadfully."

She managed a brief insincere smile. "Sorry, Sylvia," she said emphasising her name as she air kissed both her cheeks.

"Come in," Sylvia said, pulling the door open wider. "You're early. Calum called to say he'll be a little late."

So she wasn't important enough that she warranted a phone call? "Oh, he must have lost my number," she said sweetly as she followed Sylvia into the spacious hallway.

"Don't be so tetchy, Lauren. It really doesn't suit you."

Sylvia lingered in front of a full-length mirror, and finger combed her reddish brown bob. Lauren steadied herself, waiting for the onslaught of blame she imagined Sylvia couldn't wait to apportion to her.

Eyeing her through the reflection of the mirror, Sylvia said, "I don't know what's going on between you two, but I don't want to get involved."

Lauren waited for the "but whatever has happened is all your fault" speech. Instead, Sylvia shocked her when she said, "You're grown adults now, and it's time you both started acting as such. Running away is no way to conduct a marriage. It's very childish!"

Lauren stared back at her in amazement. Had Sylvia inadvertently said Calum was somehow to blame? Despite this, she had a horrible feeling that Sylvia was up to no good. She never sided with anyone but her golden boy – ever!

Lauren remained silent. The less she said, the better for everyone.

With a bemused look on her face, Sylvia continued, "Anyway, I'm going to get ready, my guests will be here soon. You know where everything is, make yourself at home."

She turned away and headed up the grand staircase.

Lauren crossed the hall and strolled into the living room. Despite being such an enormous space, it felt warm and snug as a log fire blazed in the open fireplace. Her eyes were immediately drawn to an area next to the oversized leather sofa. Piled neatly on top of each other were the stash of belongings Calum had taken when he had left their home. At first she was buoyed by the fact he hadn't unpacked his stuff, which could only mean he wasn't planning on staying there long. That theory was soon dashed as she warmed her hands in front of the searing heat and glanced up to see a pretty card with a love heart on the front. Out of curiosity, she picked it up and looked inside – expecting to see a soppy message from Calum's mum to his dad or vice versa. What she didn't expect to see was the card addressed to Calum. She scanned the words that were scrawled inside – I hope you enjoy me as much as I'm going to enjoy you! Isabella.

The nerve ends of her fingers tingled as the card slipped to the floor.

"Isabella? Who the hell is Isabella?" Hearing the sound of footsteps nearing the living room door, she scooped the card up from the floor and replaced it on the mantelpiece.

"You haven't got yourself a drink. What will it be? Wine? G and T? Or something stronger?" Sylvia asked with a smirk as she stood in the doorway, glancing from the card to Lauren with obvious satisfaction.

Lauren looked at her in dismay. How could she

be so sick? The mean hearted gesture from Sylvia hurt her more than she cared to admit. Why would Sylvia want to toy with her emotions when all she had ever done was love her son and been a supportive wife? Was she really such a threat that Sylvia wanted to destroy any feelings Lauren had left for him?

"Do you want to take your coat off? You're not outside any more, after all."

Lauren straightened her shoulders and blinked back the tears that threatened to fall.

"No need. I'm not staying. Do me a favour will you? Tell your precious son I've had a change of heart."

"Do you think that's a good idea? Maybe it's in your best interests to wait."

Lauren brushed past Sylvia in the doorway. "I've had a lot of good ideas, Sylvia. Unfortunately, coming here today was not one of them. You've proved your point, well done." She forced a smile onto her lips. "You've won. Don't worry, I won't be bothering Calum again. You can keep him."

Before Sylvia could respond, Lauren fled the room and ran down the pathway, the tears finally free to flow down her cheeks.

Eight years of her life had gone up in smoke in one act of betrayal. *An affair.* Once upon a time she would have thought that was the most outlandish thing anyone could have said about Calum. He had his faults like she had, but she would never have pegged him for the cheating type. Never in a million years. Well, it was all over now. She had gone looking for answers, and she'd found them, even if it wasn't what she was expecting.

She fumbled in her jacket for her phone. With a trembling finger she scrolled down her list of contacts and pressed a number.

"I need to see you ... now!" was all she said into the phone when her call was finally answered.

***

Twenty minutes later Lauren walked into Robin's bar and spotted Gillian sitting on a stall, sipping a drink. When Gillian caught sight of Lauren, she rested her drink on the bar and strode over to her.

Gillian gave her a brief hug. "Are you okay? You sounded dreadful on the phone."

Lauren shook her head with a wan smile. "I'll tell you in a bit. I just need a drink right now."

"Of course, of course." Gillian held Lauren around her waist and guided her back to the bar. "Robin, a double brandy, please. No ice."

Robin gave them the once over but said nothing. She poured out the drink and put it in front of Lauren.

"Thank you," Lauren mumbled as she took a mouthful and inhaled deeply as the alcohol soothed her nerves.

"Whoa, slow down," Gillian said as she brought Lauren's hands down. "You're going to make yourself sick."

Her voice shook with anger when she spoke. "I

hope so," she said, pushing aside Gillian's hands and taking another gulp.

"Okay then," Gillian said, sitting back on her stool.

Lauren turned to face her, and on the verge of tears said, "I'm sorry; I didn't mean to take it out on you."

Gillian smiled. "If you want to use me as a punch bag feel free. Just no kicking. I have to draw the line somewhere."

Lauren took a deep breath. "I just found out why Calum left me."

"And?"

Lauren cast her eyes downward. "He's been seeing another woman. Maybe he should go on a double date with my dad."

Gillian leaned back in shock. "That's worse than I thought. But what's your dad got to do with anything?"

Lauren tapped her fingernail against the glass. "Oh, nothing and everything."

"How so?" Gillian asked patiently.

Lauren took another long sip of her drink and put it back on the counter for a refill. "The money that's gone missing ..."

Gillian nodded as Robin poured another measurement in Lauren's glass.

"Well, it seems my dad's been parking his car in someone else's garage."

Gillian's eyes widened. "Do you mean?"

"Yes, that's exactly what I mean," Lauren said nodding as she brought the drink to her lips and took a long gulp. She was starting to feel much better now.

Gillian put a comforting hand on her shoulder. "Lauren, that's awful. On both counts. I'm speechless."

"The worst thing is, they've been keeping secrets from Mum and I for ages, and we didn't even realise it." She heard her bitterness spill over into her voice. "If he hadn't been fiddling the books, Mum would never have found out. And if I hadn't arrived early at Calum's parents' house, I'd never have seen the card from his new woman. I would have been left to think that it was all my fault, that I was damaged goods." The words stumbled out of her mouth in quick succession.

"You're not damaged, Lauren." Gillian gently squeezed her shoulder. "Believe me, you're far from it."

Lauren slipped out of her jacket. "I'd like another brandy, please. I want to forget all about this crappy day."

Gillian caught Robin's attention and nodded to Lauren's glass. "Same again please, Robin."

"Coming right up," she said with a sympathetic smile.

Lauren tried to smile back, but her cheeks felt as if they were weighed down with a tonne of cement. She gratefully took the glass when it was handed back to her.

"Thanks," she said as she glanced around the bar

and widened her eyes as if seeing the place for the first time. Large pictures of scantily clad women in sexually explicit poses, hung on the walls. The man in a suit a couple of seats away from them, on closer inspection, was actually a woman. "Is this a …"

"Gay bar," Gillian finished for her. "Yes, you look surprised."

"I am, it looks just like …" She tilted her head, struggling to find the right words. "Like …"

"Any other bar? That's because it is. Just because we're lesbians doesn't mean we live in a parallel universe."

Lauren hiccupped and leaned into Gillian. "I know that silly. I didn't mean to insult you."

Gillian laughed. "Don't worry, you didn't. Come on, let's go somewhere a little more private," she said picking up their drinks and leading her over to a booth in a dimly lit corner.

Lauren slid along the seat to the middle. She rested her chin in her hand and let out a long sigh. "Are you here by yourself? I haven't interrupted anything have I?"

"No, you haven't and yes I'm here by myself."

Lauren looked at Gillian with a wry smile. "Good for you. Do you know I've never been to a bar for a drink alone. Calum always said it was too dangerous," she said laughing at the ridiculousness of it all. She hadn't realised how much he had stifled her. He didn't like her doing much, it seemed, except being at his beck and call when he demanded it.

Gillian looked down as she ran the tip of her finger around the rim of her glass. "Some bars are."

"But it wouldn't stop you going into one though would it?" Lauren knew the answer before Gillian replied. No, it wouldn't because Gillian was an independent woman. Lauren couldn't see her bowing down to a man's demands. Far from it – she looked the type to tell him to stick his requests where the sun didn't shine. Maybe she should take a leaf out of Gillian's book.

"No," Gillian said carefully as she lifted her gaze. "But that's only because I like to be reckless."

Lauren inched closer to her. "Do you? What does it feel like?"

Gillian raised her brows questioningly. "Being reckless?"

Lauren nodded. Her head was spinning, but, funnily enough, she was still in charge of her senses. Her mind was clear enough to remember what was important; Calum was a cheating control freak, and she was better off without him.

"Being reckless," Gillian continued, "makes you feel alive, like you can do anything, become anyone." She rested her head against the seat and stared up towards the ceiling.

Lauren let out an exaggerated sigh. "That's what I want. Remember what we were talking about today. That's what I was trying to get at. I don't want to think about the consequences of my actions. It must be great being a psychopath. Imagine what kind of life you could lead by not having a conscience. No guilt. No regret. Just thinking about pleasing yourself every day of this miserable life."

Gillian turned her head towards Lauren and grinned. "Hey, things don't have to be that drastic. You don't have to be a psychopath to feel that way. You just have to learn to not be afraid to let go."

"Oh yeah, and how do you do that when you've been brainwashed from birth always to think of others – never yourself?"

"You just re-programme your thoughts. No one can control what you think, Lauren. It's all down to you."

Lauren moved closer, so she was leaning right up against Gillian's arm.

"Can I tell you a secret?" Lauren whispered in her ear.

Gillian laughed. "As long as you won't regret it when you're sober."

Lauren shook her head vigorously. "No way. I'm living my life guilt-free from now on."

"Okay, only if you're sure."

Lauren leaned in again. Her hazy mind was debating whether to tell Gillian how she felt. To bare her soul might prove to be her downfall. *Sod it. What's the worst thing that can happen?*

"I've been fantasizing about you ever since I bumped into you on the train."

Gillian's eyes widened. "You have?"

"Yep," Lauren quickly answered, then paused.

"And it was the best sex I've ever had." The effects of the alcohol were loosening her tongue, but she didn't care. She wanted to tell Gillian everything about herself until she knew her inside out. She didn't want any secrets between them. Secrets only hurt people, and she'd never want to hurt Gillian.

Letting out a low whistle, Gillian said, "Well, I'm very impressed with my imaginary self." She took Lauren's glass from her hand, holding her gaze, and placed it beside her own. "Can I let you into a secret of my own?"

Lauren nodded, mesmerised by her green eyes.

"I wish it hadn't all been in your head."

Lauren gasped. "You don't?"

Gillian smiled and shook her head slowly. "No. In fact, I wish I could have been inside your mind with you."

Lauren couldn't help but grin. "You do? So where does that leave us now?"

Gillian looked at her thoughtfully before saying in a regretful tone. "Exactly where we were a minute ago. You're married–"

"–Soon to be divorced," Lauren interrupted as she took another sip of brandy.

"And by the looks of it," Gillian said, "on your way to getting very drunk."

"Not drunk, Gillian." She pressed her weight against her. "Just very reckless."

Gillian laughed.

Lauren drew back and wrinkled her forehead.

"Am I a joke to you?"

Gillian shook her head. "No, not at all. You're just very cute when you're trying to be seductive."

"Oh, well how about this then." She leaned in and wrapped her hand around the back of Gillian's neck, pulling her closer and pressing her lips against Gillian's unsuspecting mouth. Lauren's head swooned back and forth upon contact, which totally caught her by surprise. She drew back a little and tried to focus her eyes. "Is that seductive enough for you?" Lauren whispered, shocked and excited by her own actions.

"Hmmm." Gillian's tongue swept over her lips. "You're going to have to try a little bit harder than that I'm afraid. After all, it sounds like I've got quite a reputation to live up to." Her eyes dropped to Lauren's breasts unashamedly.

"And there's nothing worse than a tarnished reputation is there?" Lauren said, enjoying the flirty banter.

Gillian merely smiled, her eyes expressing more of a challenge than curiosity. "No, there isn't."

With a confidence Lauren found enthralling, Gillian slowly moved her hand above the hem of Lauren's skirt.

Lauren's eyes darted around the bar as she began to feel herself getting wetter and wetter. Within seconds, Gillian had snaked her hand up her thigh, and her fingers were caressing her slowly and tenderly as she inched her way further. Lauren pressed her bottom lip between her teeth, as Gillian's hand stopped suddenly. *So near.* She inhaled Gillian's sweet scent and let out a measured breath.

"Is this what you were fantasizing about," Gillian asked, her voice low and husky.

Lauren gulped a mouthful of air and nodded. "Yes," she said in a strangled voice.

"What would you do to me if you had me in your bed right now?" she murmured, staring hard into Lauren's eyes. "I know what I'd like to do to you."

Lauren felt a jolt of electricity flash between her legs as Gillian's fingers began working her.

"Would you be shocked if I told you that I want to fuck you right now?" Gillian said.

Lauren squirmed impatiently in her seat, her heart in her mouth. Momentarily rendered speechless as a wave of excitement and hysteria washed over her. As much as she wanted Gillian, this was new territory for her, and she was way out of her comfort zone as she briefly wondered whether Gillian would be put off by her lack of experience. She wasn't sure that she could handle another knock back so soon. However, the more Gillian brazenly made circular movements against Lauren's clit with her thumb, the more her fears faded. She couldn't believe another woman had managed to get her juices flowing in just a few seconds. Lauren felt as though she was going to go insane when Gillian abruptly withdrew her hand and rose to her feet. "Get up."

In a trance-like state, Lauren complied, standing obediently and gazing longingly at Gillian, as she waited for further instructions.

"See that door over there?"

Lauren nodded, not trusting herself to speak.

"We're going through it."

A surge of adrenaline coursed through her veins as hand in hand, they walked out into the narrow, dimly lit alleyway. Lauren was used to exiting via the front door of wine bars, and as her eyes surveyed the rubbish bins that were lined up against the wall opposite, and drank in the dank, depressing surroundings, she smiled expectantly at Gillian. Her senses were in overdrive, as she savoured every last nano-second of this moment with the woman who she knew was about to turn her life upside down, in the nicest way possible.

"Do you have any idea how beautiful you are?" Gillian whispered as she pushed Lauren tenderly up against the door.

Lauren pinched her lower lip between her teeth. "Mmm … tell me," she said, loving the silky feel of Gillian's hair as it trailed through her fingers.

"Everything about you is so perfect. From the softness of your skin to the colour of your eyes." Gillian gently kissed each of her cheeks then licked a trail down one side of her neck and up the other.

Lauren's body stiffened, her muscles contracting. "What about my lips?" She was gaining in confidence now; her voice was rough with desire, husky and passionate.

"Your lips are divine. God-given for one purpose."

"What purpose?" she whispered, barely audible.

"My kisses." Gillian covered Lauren's lips with her own, pressing hard. Her tongue darting inquisitively into her mouth. Startled by how natural this felt, Lauren responded with a passion she never thought possible. Feeling truly liberated for the first time in her life, Lauren seized the moment, her trembling fingers pulling open her own shirt, suddenly grateful for the fact that she had chosen to go braless.

Gillian's head jerked back in surprise as her eyes skimmed Lauren's small and perfect breasts.

"I thought you wanted to fuck me?" Lauren whispered sexily, inwardly pleased by Gillian's reaction and grateful for the fact that, in spite of Gillian's obvious experience, she wasn't the only one struggling to control her mounting excitement.

A dirty smile spread across Gillian's face as she slowly trailed one hand the length and breadth of Lauren's body. She explored every gorgeous inch of her, from the curve of her neck, the outline of her breast, to her taut stomach, in a long, slow agonising tease. Each stroke a never-ending line of pure ecstasy across every nerve. Her hand snaked between Lauren's thighs and along the seam of her slit, the moisture coating her fingers instantly. Her probing fingers left no inch untouched, no sensation unawakened as she manipulated her clit with her palm, thumb, and fingers.

Lauren turned her head to the side and inhaled sharply. "I want you to fuck me, not tease me," she groaned.

Covering her mouth again, in a long, lingering kiss, Gillian kicked Lauren's legs apart, before sliding her middle finger inside of her. Gently exploring at first, before pushing it deep, as far as it would go. As Lauren begged for more, Gillian thrust a further three fingers inside, finger-fucking her with an intensity that Lauren hadn't known existed, all the while working Lauren's clit with her thumb. The pain of her back rubbing against the rough door, only added to Lauren's enjoyment, and as she frantically slid up and down Gillian's neatly manicured fingers, Lauren thought that she was going to go out of her mind with joy. She had fantasized about this moment ever since their chance encounter on the train. The fact that her fantasy was now reality, was almost as intoxicating as actually having sex. Almost, but not quite, and as Gillian rolled Lauren's nipple between her teeth, gently pulling, all the while fucking her hard with her fingers, Lauren thought she was going to explode. Arching back against the door, she felt all of the pent up anger and frustration that had been building over the past few days begin to melt away, as she gave herself completely to this woman and this moment.

"This is even better than I imagined … please don't stop."

"Shhh, it's going to get even better, I promise," Gillian whispered.

Lauren didn't know how much longer she could contain her orgasm as Gillian dropped to her knees, reached under her skirt and tugged her knickers down her legs. Her mouth greedily closed in on Lauren's wetness; her tongue worked furiously as her fingers squeezed and massaged Lauren's firm arse, whipping her up into a frenzy. She licked Lauren's labia up and down, then pushed her tongue deep into her, where her fingers had been just moments earlier. Lauren pulled Gillian close, her mind struggling to process the feelings of raw desire that had rendered her helpless. Biting down hard on her bottom lip to stop herself from screaming out, she bucked and moaned, "Ohh … I'm cuming," she murmured, squeezing Gillian's face.

"Oh yesss …" with a fevered groan, she dug her fingers into Gillian's hair as the earth fell away beneath her feet, and powerful tremors of ecstasy surged through her body. She tilted her head backwards and squeezed her eyes shut as her body trembled from the aftershock.

"Oh my …"

"Shhh." Gillian hissed as she stood up and placed two forefingers, which were still wet with her juices, against Lauren's lips.

All at once, Lauren heard footsteps. She froze as they both turned to watch the figure of a man stagger up the alley. Clearly drunk, he turned to the wall, took a quick piss and then disappeared out of sight.

Her heart still pounding, Lauren hastily bent down and pulled her knickers up. "Do you think he saw us?"

Gillian pressed against her. "No." Her hand crept

between her thighs. "So what do you want to do now?" she asked suggestively.

Lauren who was still burning with desire, whispered, "Can we go back to your place?"

"My place?" Gillian asked. "Are you sure?"

Lauren nodded.

"Is everything okay?"

Lauren beamed. "Yes, everything is perfect." She pulled Gillian's face towards hers and kissed her with all the passion her body possessed. Breaking away momentarily, she said breathlessly. "I … I want to make love to you."

Chapter Twenty-Three

Gillian pushed the door open to her spacious living room and pulled Lauren in behind her. "Is this okay?" Gillian asked, as she nodded towards the sofa. "Or would you prefer something a little more conventional, like a bed?"

Lauren wrapped her arms around Gillian's waist. "The sofa's fine. A bed's for sleeping on and, believe me, I have no intention of sleeping tonight."

Gillian laughed. "You are so naughty."

"Only with you."

Gillian reached to turn the light off.

"No, don't. I want to see everything,"

"The light is hurting my eyes," Gillian said as she turned the dimmer down fully.

Lauren wrapped her arm around Gillian's neck and pulled her in close. Resuming their kiss from the cab, Lauren took charge and claimed Gillian's mouth, finding her tongue and wrestling with it.

Gillian was so different from Calum. Whereas Calum was hard and muscular, Gillian was soft and delicate. Tonight, Lauren needed a rose. She needed softness and light. Needed and craved it. Tonight had been a long time in the making. Lauren had always known that she was "different." That she was mostly attracted to girls. However, she had spent so long suppressing her true feelings that she had lost sight of who she was. That was until Gillian had entered her life. Now, as she cupped Gillian's head in the palms of her hands, and kissed her, she realised that for the first time in her life, she was in control. That while there were still lingering issues from her marriage that needed to be resolved, for tonight at least, Gillian was hers to love as she pleased.

Gillian responded by shoving Lauren back over the edge of the sofa and onto the cushions. She fell with her legs spread in the air.

Lauren laughed and tried to upright herself.

Gillian moved quickly, grasped both of her ankles and stood between her thighs.

"Don't move," she ordered. Lauren lifted her head and was turned on by her dominance. Lauren forced herself to be still, as Gillian traced a line up her leg, from her ankle to the top of her thigh. Reaching the hot, juicy spot between her legs, she gently applied more pressure, slowly running her fingers back and forth over Lauren's entrance, which was by now swollen and engorged. It took every bit of willpower that Lauren possessed to avoid squirming. She could feel the moisture leaking through the fabric of her knickers again as Gillian kept on rubbing. Groaning, Lauren thrashed her head from side to side. She was too warm, too sensitive, too aroused to focus on anything else. She needed to be naked, to feel Gillian's body moulded against her own. Gillian must have sensed it because she suddenly moved away, and Lauren immediately yearned for her touch.

"Undress." The command while barely a whisper,

was clear.

Longing to regain the initiative, but unable to refuse Gillian anything that she wanted, Lauren slowly rose from the sofa. She quickly undressed and waited as Gillian slowly peeled her clothes off. From what Lauren could make out in the semi-darkness, her body was well toned and strong.

Gillian sat down on the edge of the sofa while Lauren remained standing. Stretching out upon the cushions, Gillian exposed herself to Lauren's curious gaze. Lauren watched spellbound as the darkness failed to hide Gillian slowly caressing herself.

"Do you want to taste me?" Gillian asked in a low voice.

Heady with excitement for the woman who had, up until an hour ago, only existed in her mind, Lauren nodded enthusiastically, only growing apprehensive as she neared her. She had often wondered what a woman would taste like. Wondering and doing, were two very different things though. In all of her fantasies, she had been on the receiving end, and she was scared that she wouldn't know what to do. As soon as she buried her face between Gillian's thighs, her fears disappeared and her tongue took on a mind of its own. Stroking, caressing and teasing Gillian's swollen clit with long, slow firm strokes. Making love to Gillian was as natural as breathing air. It was as if she'd been making love to women all her life. She was amazed by the smoothness of Gillian's shaven lips as she dropped small kisses on the moist warm folds between her thighs.

Without warning, Gillian pushed her to the ground and straddled her, positioning herself so that she was just inches away from Lauren's face. Instinctively, Lauren anchored her hands around Gillian's hips and pulled her down onto her mouth, her tongue darting and diving into Gillian's wet folds, causing her lover to jerk forward onto all fours.

Gillian let out an unadulterated scream of pleasure as using mouth and tongue, Lauren bit, suckled and probed her. Feeling more confident than she could have ever imagined, she reached up and grabbed Gillian's breasts. Squeezing them hard as Gillian ground her clit onto Lauren's tongue, thrusting her hips back and forth in a steady rhythm.

Lauren had never thought that sex could be so exhilarating in real life. She found herself wanting this moment to never end. The more excited Gillian became, the more Lauren found herself wanting to lose herself in her forever, as her own clit pulsated and tingled with pleasure.

Gillian grasped Lauren's hands in her own, pressing them hard against her breasts as she bucked wildly, letting out a strangled groan as her body shuddered, and her juices flowed into Lauren's open mouth.

"That," Gillian said, trying to catch her breath, "was fucking amazing."

"Yes, it was," Lauren said, her own body aching for release again.

Gillian's breasts rose and fell with each laboured breath as she seamlessly switched position and covered Lauren's body with her own.

"Wow, you are hot aren't you?" A limpid expression of desire glowed in her eyes.

Lauren squirmed beneath her. "And impatient." She laughed nervously. "I'm sorry but I'm going to scream if you don't fuck me again soon." The words had left her lips before she had time to process them.

Gillian traced the outline of her breast as she took a deep long breath. "Well, I'd better get started hadn't I?"

Bending her knee, she spread Lauren's legs apart, fitted her thigh tight into her crux and began moving up and down. She slid her hands over Gillian's smooth arse and gripped her cheeks tightly as Gillian continued the slow and steady motion, rubbing her engorged clit up and down; the sensation sending bolts of pleasure straight to her core. Her breath caught in her throat. As if sensing her oncoming explosion, Gillian moved down to the softness between her thighs. Widening her legs, she swept the tip of her tongue over Lauren's clit with a rapid circular movement, increasing and decreasing the pressure alternately. Lauren's body quaked with desire as her clit became more sensitive with every stroke of Gillian's tongue. For the second time that night, Gillian slid her fingers into her. It was the only catalyst needed to send waves of ecstasy pulsating through her body. Leaving her fingers inside her, despite Lauren's seizing climax, she thrust them in and out until Lauren was moaning so loudly she barely recognised the sound of her own voice.

Oh … my … God …! Lauren expelled her breath in a slow, steady hiss as she wiped a film of perspiration from her forehead with the back of her hand. *Un–fucking-believable*!

Goose pimples covered her skin as Gillian worked her way back up her body with a trail of small kisses. Reaching her side she leaned over and gently pushed her hair away from her face.

"So, did I live up to your fantasy?" she asked teasingly, as a mischievous smile formed on her lips.

Lauren tried to open her eyes, but her lids were too heavy. "Hmmm, I'll have to let you know later. You've only fulfilled two of my many fantasies," she said sleepily, as she pulled Gillian to her and buried her face in her hair. She had never wanted to be inside someone's skin so badly.

As she lay there, sweaty and spent, a small voice in the back of her mind warned her to pull away from the situation before things got too complicated. As she felt the stirrings of desire mounting from the touch of Gillian's hand caressing her breast, she realised that her body's voice was much louder than the voice of reason. That's why she made a conscious decision to ignore it.

Chapter Twenty-Four

"Shut the door, Ken," Jean said as she sat down on the sofa with a glass of chardonnay. She had been waiting for the right moment to approach him about her findings, but was there ever a right time to call your husband a thief? She was not an emotional woman, but the thought that Ken, her husband of thirty years, could so easily betray her brought a lump to her throat.

Ken ignored her request and instead walked to the middle of the room and stood with his hands behind his back. "I wish you wouldn't talk to me like a child, especially when Lauren's around. No wonder she's losing respect for me."

"Well, if you didn't act like one half the time," she crossed her legs, "I wouldn't have to would I?"

He frowned at her over his half-moon shaped glasses. "What's this about Jean? You've got Lauren in a right state. What is it you've accused me of now?"

"Where shall we start?" Jean said with a smile. "Oh yes, how about the missing money."

Ken removed his glasses and stuffed his hand into his trouser pocket. Retrieving a white hanky, he began to clean his glasses. "What missing money?" he asked innocently, keeping his focus on the job at hand.

Jean reached over to the coffee table and picked up the file resting on it. He wouldn't be able to refute her claims now that she had actual proof of his indiscretions, no matter how hard he tried to talk himself out of it. She threw the folder towards him, the pages scattering on the floor by his feet.

Jean rose from her seat. "It's all in there. Everything you've stolen, down to the last penny." For the first time in her life, she experienced the raw feeling of hate. Why he would have put her in this position, she didn't know.

Ken let out a heavy sigh as he replaced his glasses on the bridge of his nose and looked at her. "I don't know what you're talking about."

"Oh, just give it up, Ken," she snapped angrily. "For God's sake. Don't you know when you're beaten?"

His voice sounded jumpy when he spoke. "I don't–"

Jean held up her hand. "–Okay, okay so you didn't take the money. Well, in that case someone in our Surrey branch is a thief." She walked over to the telephone and picked it up.

"What are you doing?" he asked in a panicked voice.

"What do you think? I'm calling the police. You don't think I'm going to let someone get away with this, do you?" she said as she slowly punched in the first number.

Ken rushed over to her and put his hand over Jean's. "Put the phone down, Jean."

She looked up at him questioningly. "Why?"

"Because …" his voice trailed off.

"Because what Ken? Just bloody tell me. Be a

man for once in your godforsaken life."

It was a couple of seconds before he replied. When he did his voice was apologetic and husky with emotion, his eyes misty with tears. "Alright, alright, I took the money, okay."

Jean closed her eyes and inhaled a deep breath. She counted to ten in her head. If she was going to get to the bottom of his deceit she had to remain as calm as humanly possible, given the circumstances. "Are you going to tell me why you took it?" She couldn't bring herself to look at him. If she did, she wouldn't be held accountable for her actions.

"You won't understand, Jean."

She paused for a second trying to keep her voice on an even keel. "You'll never know unless you try."

Jean turned away from him and walked back to the sofa. Her legs were weak, and her hands trembled as she sat down again and reached for her drink. She steeled herself as she waited for his confession. In her heart she knew there had to be another woman involved, there had to be. How else could he explain stealing so much money? She waited patiently as he took a bottle of whisky from the drinks cabinet and poured himself a generous amount. After taking a mouthful, he set the glass on the cabinet and turned to her.

"I bought a flat," he said in a monotone.

Jean jerked back, completely stunned. If he had said he'd been to the moon, she couldn't have been more gobsmacked. "You bought a flat? With money you stole from me?"

Ken looked at her in confusion. "I didn't steal it. It's our money, Jean. I'm entitled to it as well."

Jean stared at him. She felt her stomach plummet. The situation was far worse than she'd feared. He actually thought he was in the right. That he bore absolutely no responsibility for his actions.

"Do you believe a court would agree with that statement when they find out what lengths you went to in order to cover your tracks? Does what you've done sound like the actions of an innocent man?"

Ken blinked rapidly. "What do you mean a court?"

She narrowed her eyes. "Do you think I'm going to roll over and take this with a pinch of salt? If you do, you're more of a fool than I thought."

In two strides, Ken was by the sofa, taking her hand as he knelt down in front of her. "Jean, please listen to me. I can sell the flat. You can have the money back with interest."

For one fleeting moment, she wished she could have a cigarette to calm her nerves, which was silly because she'd never smoked in her life. But she needed something to calm her down. This was the last straw for their relationship. He had been nothing but a drain on her finances and her emotions for too long.

She stood abruptly. "Get away from me, Ken. You repulse me!" she said moving to the other side of the room. Despite herself she needed to know his reasoning behind his actions. "Why did you do it?

Haven't I always given you everything you wanted and more? Why did you have to steal from me?"

"I just needed time for myself. As much as I love your mother, Jean, it's got too much for me having her living with us for all these years."

"And what the hell do you think it's been like for me. A sodding picnic!" Jean exhaled deeply, finally releasing her pent up tension. "You are a pathetic excuse for a man, Ken. You always have been. You've had it too easy riding on my coat tails, but that's about to stop."

"What are you going to do, Jean?" he asked, his bottom lip visibly trembling. "Please don't call the police. They'll put me away. I'd rather kill myself than go to jail," he said frantically.

She looked at him with disgust. "You know what; I actually believe you would commit such a selfish act. Why the hell I married someone like you I don't know! And to have actually had a child with someone as spineless as you."

It was only because of Lauren that she hadn't called the police and pressed charges. Even though Lauren had said she'd support any decision she made, she knew she would never forgive her if she had her father locked up. She was about to lose a husband, she didn't want to lose her daughter as well.

"Jean, please talk to me," Ken pleaded.

"You've got Lauren to thank for me not getting your arse hauled to jail. I want my money back and I want you to pack your stuff and get out of my house."

"But–"

She glared at him. "–Believe me, Ken, the less I see of you the better it will be."

Chapter Twenty-Five

A silvery streak of moonlight fought its way through the slated blinds, as the women lay entwined on the sofa, still sweaty and hot from their latest bout of love making.

Lauren pressed her cheek against Gillian's hand. "I take it you've had a lot of experience with other women?"

"I wouldn't exactly call myself Don Juan."

Lauren laughed self-consciously. "I bet they were ten times better than me."

Gillian pulled her into her arms. "Are you kidding? You were, sorry, are amazing. Believe me, you could sleep with a million women but if there isn't a connection here," she said tapping her heart. "Then it's just sex and that's it. What we've just experienced was lovemaking. There's a big difference."

A burst of happiness engulfed her. "I like that." Lauren snuggled against Gillian's chest.

"Good," Gillian said squeezing her tightly.

The sound of a mobile phone ringing startled them both. "Oh crap. I think it's mine. I'm going to have to get it." Lauren disentangled herself from Gillian's arms and legs. "It's most probably the police calling to inform me my mum's murdered my dad."

Lauren slid off the sofa and stumbled around in the dark, eventually finding her phone underneath Gillian's bra.

"Hi, Mum," Lauren said without looking at the screen.

"It's not your Mum; it's Calum." His voice was firm and impersonal.

She turned to stare in Gillian's direction tongue-tied. "Calum?"

"Yes, Calum," he replied. "I've been trying to get you all evening and your phone's been ringing and ringing. Where are you?"

She looked at the time on her phone. 23:00. "That's none of your business."

"My mum said you were rather rude and left abruptly earlier."

Lauren clenched her jaw. "Well, she would, wouldn't she? Look, Calum, what do you want? I'm kind of busy at the moment."

His voice tightened. "I'm at the house."

Lauren snorted. "Oh, really. I thought you'd be holed up with your bit on the side."

"My what?"

"Oh, don't play games with me, Calum. I saw the card on your mum's mantelpiece and the pathetic message from your tart. 'I hope you'll enjoy me as much as I'll enjoy you'," she mocked. "Does that ring a bell?"

Calum laughed, and his voice softened for the first time. "Lauren, you've got it all wrong–"

Furious, she flung the words at him like bullets. "–No, Calum, you've got it all wrong thinking I'm some kind of mug. Well, I'm not. Please don't call me again," she said with finality and ended the call.

Gillian reached down to pick up her shirt and slid her arms into it. "That went well."

Lauren stood naked in the middle of the living room. "I can't believe the nerve of him. Can you imagine someone laughing when you've just busted them?" she said scathingly.

Gillian's lips twisted into a cynical smile. "You didn't really give him a chance to explain."

"What's to explain? I saw the evidence with my own eyes. Fidelity is important to me, Gillian. Once the trust has been broken, that's the end of it for me."

Gillian leaned back and toyed with a strand of hair. "That sounds kind of hypocritical – you said you were fantasizing about me."

Lauren let out a bitter laugh. "So maybe I should go to prison for imagining robbing a bank. Fantasizing is hardly the same as shagging someone in real life."

"So, what about what we've just done?"

Lauren smiled as she walked over to her seductively. "What have we done?"

"You've just cheated on him."

She straddled Gillian's lap and caressed her neck with her tongue. "Yes, that's very true, but without sounding like I'm in the school playground, he started it first."

Gillian wrapped her arms around her waist and pulled her closer. "So this was tit for tat?" she said pulling Lauren's nipple into her mouth.

Lauren ran her fingers through Gillian's hair and

pressed her breast hard against her mouth. "No, of course not. I had no way of knowing when I came to meet you at the bar, that you were going to fuck my brains out in an alleyway," she whispered in her ear as she nibbled and licked it.

Gillian laughed. "It really is true what they say about the quiet ones being the dirtiest."

"You bet. I can't wait to show you just how dirty I can be."

Chapter Twenty-Six

Gillian rolled into the vacant space Lauren had occupied up until an hour ago. She could still smell the scent of her perfume on the pillow.

What a night and what a woman.

When the door bell sounded, she jumped out of bed, slipped into her dressing gown and hurried to open the door.

"Good morning, Travis," she said hugging him. "Is everything okay?" she asked noticing his sombre mood.

He shrugged his shoulders. "Would be better if I had one of your coffees down me."

"Coming right up."

"I thought you'd be up and about by now."

"I had a late night," she said following him through to the kitchen.

"Oooh sounds promising." He dropped into his favourite chair near the window and opened up a bag of freshly baked croissants. "Do tell."

"After you," she said pouring the coffee into a mug. "How did it go with Cody?"

"Well," he said quietly. "It turned out to be easier to find the source of my infection than I thought."

Gillian held her breath. "Travis, no!"

Travis nodded. "Yep. He's been positive for six months."

The coffee mug she was holding slipped from her

hand and dropped to the floor, steaming hot coffee splashing both her legs.

Travis leapt out of his seat, grabbed a sheet of kitchen roll and ran over to her with it. "Let me help you," he said bending down and dabbing her legs dry.

She clamped her hand over his and pulled him up. "Travis. Did you know he was positive?

Travis pulled his face. "What do you think?"

"And he didn't tell you. Jesus Christ, what kind of sick bastard is he?"

"He thought if we had safe sex I wouldn't get it."

Gillian couldn't believe what she was hearing. "Wasn't that your choice to make? Jesus, Travis, how can you be so blasé about this?"

Travis shrugged. "Do you think jumping up and down and throwing my toys out the pram, is going to make the virus disappear? Gillian, I've been working with people with HIV for twenty years. I've heard all kinds of stories, witnessed deaths more times than I'd care to remember as well as all the miracles," he added with a smile. "I knew all the risks. Yes, Cody was wrong not to tell me–"

"–Are you kidding me, wrong? Wrong is when you forget an anniversary or your mother's birthday. It's not wrong to not disclose your status, it's downright criminal."

"He never intentionally put me in any danger."

"So how did you get it, from the toilet seat?" she asked incredulously. "Fucking hell, Travis, what's wrong with you? This man hasn't given you a cold;

he's given you a life sentence." She immediately regretted the words as soon as they'd left her mouth. "Oh Travis, I'm sorry."

He held up his hand. "Don't be. I can understand your anger. If I were a young twenty-something, I'd probably feel that way as well. But I'm almost twice your age and without meaning to sound patronising; I've experienced a hell of a lot of things that have shaped the way I look at the world. I'm sure he would have got round to telling me in his own time."

"Oh, that's fantastic. So all is forgiven, and you're going to just forget all about it and live happily ever after?"

"That's exactly what I'm going to do. I love him, whether that makes me an idiot I don't know, but I can't help the way I feel."

"It's your call, Travis. Like I told you from the beginning, I'll support you with whatever you decide to do. But that doesn't mean I think it's okay what he did."

Travis looked doubtful for a few moments then he grinned. "I think Cody had better keep his front to you when he finally meets you, especially if there are any knives around … Oh, sorry that was in poor taste, but you know what I mean."

"Nothing can be worse than what you've just told me." Gillian opened a cupboard and took a broom out to clear the broken mug. The tears welling in her eyes spilled onto her cheeks.

Travis pushed her hair away from her face.

"Hey, you're cheating, we said no more tears. Come on, dry them," he said pulling a tissue from his breast pocket.

"I'm so angry on your behalf. I can't believe someone who supposedly loves you would put you in such a position."

He embraced her. "I know, but I'm a big boy, Gillian. It wasn't his fault the condom broke. Shit happens sometimes. Even if I'd known his status, how could I have prevented that night. Now forget about me. I have no intention of living, sleeping and eating HIV all the time. Now tell me, missy, why you had a late night?"

"Lauren came over," she said sheepishly as she wiped away her tears.

"Lauren? Never! How on earth did you manage to swing that?"

"I don't know actually. It was not intentional, believe me."

"Oh my God. See, you can't be let out on your own. You're too much of a liability, you little floozy," he said, playfully smacking her behind.

Gillian laughed.

"So what happens next?"

"Nothing, Travis. She's a married woman. She'll do what most of them do in this situation; go back to their husbands for one reason or another. Only this time I'm not the gullible young girl I once was." As much as she cared about Lauren, she wasn't about to let her have a free rein on her heart. It would have been a different matter if Lauren had been divorced and not in the middle of a bust-up with her husband due to infidelity issues. She had known too many people who forgave their partners and gave their relationship another go. She was in too deep already, way more than she'd ever imagined. As long as there were no promises made on either side she could deal with the consequences. That way, if Lauren decided to go back to Calum, though it would hurt, it wouldn't come as a surprise. She had made a promise to herself, all those years ago, that she would protect her heart from being broken again, and she had meant it. There was no going back on her word – not even for Lauren.

Chapter Twenty-Seven

Lauren could smell the fresh fragrance of flowers before she even opened the door to her office. As she reached for the handle, her mother appeared in the hallway with a smile on her face.

"So, you and Calum made up last night then?" Jean said as she came to a standstill in front of her.

Lauren pulled her face. She was too high in the clouds to get dragged down with her problems with Calum. "Um, no, not really. I didn't see him."

Jean's face dropped. "So, what's with the flowers?"

Lauren pushed the door open, and her eyes fell on an enormous bouquet of roses in a vase on her desk. "I don't know what he's playing at to tell you the truth." She was insulted that he thought she could be bought off with a bunch of flowers. The old Lauren well might have been. But the newly awakened Lauren was putting up with no such bullshit any more. She knew exactly what or rather who she wanted to be with and it most certainly wasn't Calum.

"Oh, come on, Lauren. Give the man a chance."

"What like you gave Dad you mean?" she said sarcastically. "He called me in tears this morning. He's scared you're going to call the police on him."

"Good. Let him have a few sleepless nights. He'll know exactly how I've been feeling these past few months." Jean walked over to the window and kept her back to Lauren.

Lauren eyed her mum suspiciously. "So you're not going to press charges?"

"No, Lauren. I'm not. Only because I don't want you caught in the middle of this."

"Thanks, Mum," Lauren said as she walked over to her and kissed her cheek. "Don't think for a minute I agree with what he's done. At least he's going to repay you once he's sold the flat."

Jean turned to face her, a slight frown on her face. "Lauren, I don't want him to sell the flat. He's going to need somewhere to live."

Lauren fell from her cloud in one big heap. "So you're getting a divorce?"

"Yes. I can't forgive your father for what he's done to me."

"I understand. You know what's best for you."

Jean narrowed her eyes. "Are you trying to make me feel better?"

"No. What he did to you was atrocious."

Jean pursed her lips. "Yes, it was."

"Exactly! And that's why I'm on your side." She wasn't going to stand in her mother's way. If she had learnt anything recently, it was to let things run their natural course. If they were meant to be together they would be. Like her mother had pointed out, she was a grown woman with her own life to get on with.

Jean tossed her head back and suddenly laughed. "Who would have thought your father committing a crime would have been the thing to finally bring us together."

"I think we've got a few more challenges ahead of us before we reach that point," Lauren said thinking ahead. She had some life changes to make and she didn't know whether her mother was going to be onboard with them or not.

The laughter faded from Jean's face as she smoothed the collar of her jacket. She looked at Lauren enquiringly. "Have you got something to tell me?"

"Not yet, Mum. When the time is right, you'll be the first to know."

Jean walked to the door. "I hope it's not going to be too long, Lauren. You've seen what happens when people keep secrets. It can tear the strongest of relationships apart."

"Yes, I know." She leaned over and sniffed the flowers.

Before leaving the room, Jean said, "At least call Calum and thank him for the flowers. If I taught you anything, it was to have good manners."

Lauren slumped onto her chair. Her feet ached, and she thought about removing her shoes but couldn't muster the energy to do so. A smile played on her lips. She only had herself to blame; no one told her to stay up until the early hours of the morning playing out all of her fantasies with the woman of her dreams. She looked at the flowers and let out a deep sigh. Why couldn't Calum just magically disappear? She didn't want to have to deal with him any more. All she wanted now was Gillian.

She took her phone from her pocket and reluctantly dialled Calum's number – it went straight to voicemail. *Surprise, surprise.* She had never contacted him at work before but she'd had enough. Opening the browser on her phone, she navigated to the hospital website and clicked on the phone number. After a couple of rings, the switchboard answered and she was transferred to the appropriate ward. "Hi, I'd like to speak to Doctor Parker, please"

Lauren opened her laptop and powered it up.

"Doctor Parker? Calum Parker?"

"Yes, that's right."

She hovered the cursor over the excel file and clicked on it.

"I'm afraid he hasn't worked here for six months."

Her heart leapt into her throat, and she fell back against her seat. "He doesn't work there?"

"No, is there anyone else I can pass you through to?"

"No, that's okay. Thanks anyway."

Lauren looked away from her computer as she disconnected the call. What the hell was going on? A new woman. Leaving the job he said was his life. Was he having a midlife crisis at twenty-five? She snapped her computer lid shut and hurried to her mum's office.

Scruff wagged his tail excitedly when he saw her. "Hey, sweetie," she said patting his head distractedly. "Look, Mum, something's come up. I need to go home for a while. Is that okay?"

Her mum didn't look up from her paperwork. "Of course. Leave Scruff here, he's keeping me company."

"Okay, thanks." Her voice trembled. She couldn't believe she'd been living with a stranger in her house for so long. Who was this man she'd once idolised?

Jean looked up and removed her glasses as she eyed her closely. "Lauren, is anything wrong?"

"I don't know. That's what I'm hoping to find out."

***

"Calum, are you here?" Lauren called out angrily as she walked through the front door. "Calum!" she raised her voice even louder.

"I'm in here," came the solemn reply from the kitchen.

She dropped her bag by the door, walked into the kitchen and straight into Calum.

"What are you doing home so early?" he asked, trying to embrace her.

She angrily brushed his arms aside. "Unless you forgot, I live here. Which reminds me, you don't."

"Come on, Lauren. Give me a break."

"A break." She laughed with bitterness. "How about you give me the fucking truth for once in your life." She was breathless with rage.

Calum looked at her in confusion. "Calm down. I don't know what you're talking about?"

Lauren snorted. "Oh, just drop the fucking act,

Calum. I know all of your secrets now. The woman you've been seeing, the fact that you left the hospital six months ago."

Calum's jaw dropped open. "How did you know?" he stammered in bewilderment.

"I called your work, sorry your ex-workplace. They told me you left six months ago. You obviously didn't want to be a doctor any more. Pretty much the same way you decided you didn't want to be my husband any more," she said with a snarky smile.

He shook his head. "I never said that, Lauren. This isn't about you."

Lauren threw her hands in the air and began pacing the floor to try and work off the excess energy. She felt as if she was going to explode. "No, it seems it's not. It's all about you isn't it? Where you want to live, when you want to have sex, where you need to be for work, or not as the case may be. The last eight years have been nothing but about you."

"Come on, Lauren."

She stopped abruptly and stared him down. "No, I won't. I want to say my piece. I've waited long enough to say it!" She walked over and sat down. "How is it that you get to decide you don't want to be a doctor? After me having to put my life on hold all these years." There was a cold edge to her voice.

He looked away hastily. "I thought it was what I wanted–"

Her face clouded with anger. "You thought?"

"Look, are you going to let me speak or not?"

His voice drifted into a hushed whisper.

For a second she thought he was going to cry. But he looked at her with dry pleading eyes.

She glared at him. "Talk and I'm telling you it had better be good."

Calum sat down and held his head in his hands. "All my life I've done what's expected of me. My dad pressured me to aim higher and achieve more. Go to University; get a good degree, find yourself an attentive wife." He looked up at her apologetically. "All this time it was as if I was a puppet on a string, doing my master's bidding. Then, at Aunt Frieda's funeral last year, as I watched her being lowered into the ground I thought – is that it? All the stresses and strains in life end with you being lowered into the earth. It's as if I had an epiphany right then and there at the edge of the grave. I just knew I couldn't carry on with my life the way it had been going."

"But why didn't you tell me you were feeling this way?"

He spoke tentatively. "Because I didn't want to disappoint you. I saw how proud you were when you introduced me as your doctor husband."

She cleared her throat. "But, Calum, that was nothing to do with my dreams or aspirations. I was proud of you because I thought you were doing what you'd wanted to do all your life. I couldn't have cared less if you were a cleaner as long as you were happy."

He smiled wryly. "Yeah, well I was too caught up in my big ego to see the truth."

"So where have you been going all this time and where've you been getting your money?"

"From my mum. I've been trying to figure out how to tell you." He stood, walked over to her and knelt by her side. "I'm really sorry that I underestimated your love for me."

"Is that why you've been having an affair?"

Calum started to laugh. She threw him a warning glance, and he stopped abruptly.

"I don't know why you seem to think infidelity is so funny."

"It's not. You've got the wrong end of the stick on that one."

"Calum, I saw the card. Are you trying to imply I was seeing things? It was all in my imagination?"

"No, of course not. The card was from my mum."

"Do you think I'm stupid? It was signed Isabella, not Sylvia."

"Yes, because Isabella is the boat my mum just bought me!"

She was baffled. "She bought you a boat?"

"Yes, and she's called Isabella. As if I'd ever be unfaithful to you."

Lauren wanted to disappear into a large gaping hole. "So why did you leave?"

Her stomach churned with anxiety and frustration at the way the conversation was going. It looked like she had jumped the gun. She should have known better than to have been taken in by his mother's games.

He bowed his head. "I left because I couldn't take lying to you any more, but I wasn't brave enough to tell you the truth until now." He took her hands in his. "Do you forgive me for lying?"

She drew back her hands and stood. "Calum, this is a lot to digest."

"Do you want me to come home so we can sort things out?" he asked hopefully.

She swallowed hard, trying her best to sound sincere. "Why don't you stay at your mum's a bit longer? I need space to think."

"If that's what you want."

Mixed feelings surged through her. "It is. I'm going to have to go back to work. Let yourself out when you're ready."

Chapter Twenty-Eight

The enormity of what she had done with Gillian hit her like a tornado. She had broken her vows due to a misunderstanding. *Oh God, why didn't he just tell me the truth in the beginning before things got out of hand*? What was she going to do now? Fess up and hope Calum could find it in his heart to forgive her? Or carry on with her soul searching journey?

Now that she had tasted the forbidden fruit, could she ever go back to being Calum's wife? What did he want out of life now if he didn't want to be a doctor? It was as if she didn't know him at all. All she knew was that she had never, in all her life, had someone made her feel so complete, so amazing, so alive as Gillian had.

She needed to talk about it, and there was only one person she could do that with. Instead of heading to the tube station she took a diversion to her father's new flat. He would understand why she wanted to break free – hadn't that been the whole purpose of him buying his own property with the money he took?

It wasn't long before she was waiting patiently outside his flat.

The door opened slightly, and Lauren caught a quick glimpse of a blonde woman before she quickly shut it again.

Oh my God, so there is another woman. Dazed, she clenched her hand into a fist and pounded on the door. She didn't care if the neighbours heard her and called the police. She wanted to confront her dad and the bitch he was holed up in there with. "Dad, I know you're in there. Open this door. I've seen her so there's no denying it any more," she shouted through the letter box.

The door opened slowly. "Come in, Lauren."

Lauren shoved the door hard, and it swung back against the wall. "Right you'd better tell me what the hell …" She turned around to look at the woman huddled against the wall with her back to her. "What the …?" she started and then closed her mouth as the woman slowly turned to face her. She was horrified by what she saw. "Dad … is that you?"

Ken raised his eyes to hers. "Yes, it's me, Lauren."

She swallowed the sick that was travelling up her throat as she gawped at the stranger before her dressed in a tight pink bodice, black leather mini-skirt, fishnet tights and knee length boots. He had failed miserably at trying to cover his five o'clock shadow with a thick layer of foundation. "But … I don't understand. Whose clothes are you wearing?"

Ken shot a nervous glance in her direction. "They're mine, Lauren. These are my clothes."

She looked at him wide-eyed. "Yours? But they're women's," she said dumbly as her brain scrambled to make sense of what she was seeing. Her heart sank.

"So the lingerie was for–"

"–Yes, it was for me."

"This is sick; it can't be happening." Embarrassed for her father and feeling at a loss for words, she turned away hurriedly and took a step towards the open door.

"Please don't go, Lauren."

The tearful desperation in his voice halted her step.

"Please stay. I need to talk to someone."

She sighed and said in a quiet voice. "I'll stay but I'm not talking to you while you're dressed like that!"

She heard his sharp intake of breath at her harsh tone of voice and immediately felt guilty. She couldn't even begin to imagine how her dad must feel having his secret life exposed to his daughter like this, but she was still reeling with shock. In her straight-laced life, she'd only ever read about men wearing their wives clothes. She would never have imagined her own father would be one of those men. *Thank God Mum's much smaller than him.* She shuddered at the thought of it.

"Okay, I'll get changed. Go and wait in the living room. It's at the end of the hall," he said closing the front door.

She would listen to what he had to say, but she still wasn't strong enough to look at him again in that outfit. With her head bowed, she walked the short distance to the room. Looking around, she wondered who had decorated the place. Pastel coloured walls, and fabric furnishings were well placed around the room. She buried her face in her hands as she thought of what it all meant. *Does this mean Dad wants to be a woman?* How on earth was her mother going to get her head around this one?

She jumped when she heard her dad's voice behind her.

"Do you want a drink, love?"

She spun around and was relieved to see he was dressed like her dad again, except for a spot or two of foundation he'd missed. It was the only tell-tale sign that she hadn't imagined it all, and it had been a horrible dream.

She nodded. "Something strong, please."

"This must be quite a shock for you, Lauren."

Lauren nodded in agreement. "That's a bit of an understatement," she blurted out.

"I'm sorry you found out this way."

"Would you have ever have told me? Does Mum know about … ?"

Ken shook his head. "No."

"So she was right about another woman, just not in the way she thought?"

"Are you going to tell her?"

"Dad, I can't pretend I like the idea of what you're doing. I don't know if I'll ever understand it, but it's your life and it's up to you if you want to share this with Mum. I've got enough of my own secrets without taking on yours," she said wearily.

"I'd prefer if you didn't say anything to her. She hates me enough as it is."

"But why do you do it? And for how long?"

He poured out two drinks and handed one to her. "Since my teens," he said with a shy smile. "And I don't know why."

"Are you … do you want to be a woman?"

He shook his head. "Contrary to popular belief, not every man who wears women's clothes wants to be a woman."

"I see," she said frowning. "I think if you told Mum the truth, at least she'd be able to understand why you took the money."

Ken shrugged. "I don't think I'm brave enough, Lauren." His voice quivered. "Are you ashamed of me?"

"No, of course I'm not," she said truthfully. "It's just a lot to take in; that's all." She walked over and hugged him. "I'm sure it's going to be fine."

Ken's arms tightened around her. "Thank you," he said in a choked voice.

When her mobile began to ring, she fished it out of her pocket and looked down at the screen.

"It's Mum. She's most probably wondering where I am. Don't worry I won't say I'm here?"

"Best not. I'd better go and sort out Kendra's clothes, in case you're mother has a change of heart and decides to call the police after all."

Lauren winced as she ignored her mother's call. She wanted to find out more about her father's secret life. "Is that what you call yourself – Kendra?"

He smiled sheepishly. "The girls down the club suggested it."

"The girls … you mean you go out in public dressed like a …" the words stuck in her throat.

"Woman, yes. You'd be surprised how many people feel the same way I do. Doctors, policemen, firefighters …"

"I bet that looks interesting," she said, trying her hardest not to think of burly hairy firefighters in dresses.

Lauren's phone rang again. "I'd better answer it," she said pressing the accept button.

"Lauren," her mother spoke quickly. "You'd better come back immediately. Scruff isn't looking too well. I think he needs to see a vet."

"What's wrong with him?"

"He's been sick and he won't stand up."

"Can you call the vet and make an emergency appointment? I'm going to grab a cab right now."

Lauren snatched her bag from the sofa. "Sorry, I've got to take Scruff to the vet." She ran out of the door and down the stairs. Without thinking, she called Calum as she hailed a taxi. It went straight to voicemail.

Damn you Calum, this is an emergency! She slammed the door behind her as she settled into the back of the cab and gave the driver the address of the shop. Her phone rang. She was relieved to think Calum had got the message and was calling back.

"Hello."

"Well, hello yourself," Gillian answered.

It took Lauren a second to recognise the voice. "Oh, Gillian."

"Nice to hear from you too," Gillian said, sounding a little hurt.

"I'm sorry," she said quickly. "I'm on my way to collect Scruff. He needs to see the vet."

"Oh no, nothing serious I hope?" Her voice was full of concern. "Where's the vet's?"

"High Street Kensington. Look, I'm going to have to call you back, Calum might be trying to get hold of me."

"Oh, okay."

By the time the taxi pulled up outside the shop, Lauren's nerves were shot. She couldn't entertain the idea of something being wrong with her precious boy. All thoughts of her personal problems would have to take a back seat for now.

"Can you wait for five minutes? I need to go somewhere else."

"Sure," the cab driver said as he turned his radio dial to a sports channel.

Lauren ran into the shop and straight to her mother's office. "Has he stood up yet?" She was frantic as she looked down at Scruff.

"No," Jean said. "He still hasn't moved from his spot."

Lauren grabbed his favourite blanket and scooped him up. For the first time ever his little tail didn't wag. "What's the matter, sweetheart?" she burrowed her head into the back of his neck. He felt so hot.

Hurrying back to the cab, she gave the address to

the driver.

"Awww, little fella looks like he doesn't feel too good," the driver said glancing at Scruff.

"No, he's not. I'm really worried about him. He's only two."

"Oh, don't worry too much, Miss. I'm sure it's nothing serious."

"I hope so."

He nodded and pulled out into the traffic. Holding Scruff against her stomach, with her free hand she texted Calum. *I'm on my way to the vet's. Can you meet me there?*

She was getting more frantic minute by minute, and she needed someone more level-headed beside her in an emergency like this. She was too emotional in these situations.

Scruff looked up at her with big sad eyes, eventually thumping his tail as tears rolled down her cheeks. Then he closed his eyes and went to sleep. The morning traffic was driving her crazy. To her they should have been in an ambulance with lights and sirens to go the vet's. *Why isn't Calum calling me back? Why does he keep switching his bloody phone off? Didn't he care about anything any more?* Maybe it had been a blessing that he'd left her when he did. For the first time, she'd seen his true colours. He really didn't give a shit about anything except what he wanted. How different Gillian was. She had heard the concern in her voice when she'd told her Scruff was ill, despite him having peed on her boot.

Finally, the cab pulled up into a vacant parking space at the vet's. Lauren was surprised to see Gillian standing outside. She walked up to the cab and opened the door, then offered her hand. Lauren grabbed hold of it and heaved herself and Scruff out of the car.

"Awww. What's up, little one?" Gillian frowned at Scruff, who just peered back at her. "Do you want to pee on my shoe? Will that make you feel better?"

Lauren laughed. It felt good to laugh for just a second.

"Take him in. I've got the cab," Gillian said as she reached into her bag for her purse.

"No, really," Lauren fumbled for her wallet.

"It's okay. Take Scruff in, the sooner we find out what's wrong with him, the better."

"Okay. Thank you, Gillian. You being here means a lot to me." She rushed towards the vet's door and pushed it open.

"Awww what's up, Scruff?" Becky, the receptionist, said when she looked at him.

"If only he could talk." Lauren was about to cry.

"Don't worry. He'll be right as rain soon. Go on through. Helena's waiting for you."

"Oh, thank you." Lauren felt better just being in the company of professionals. She hugged Scruff tight and went through the door and down the hall. Helena smiled when she entered the room and gestured for her to put Scruff on the examining table. She was in her mid-fifties and a tall, distinguished looking woman.

"Good morning, Lauren." She smiled warmly and

shook Lauren's hand.

"Morning, Helena. Thank you for seeing us so quickly."

"No worries. Let's take a look at the little fella."

Scruff perked up a bit, craning his neck to look around. Helena stroked his head while she reached for the thermometer.

"Ok, Scruff," she said, scratching him under his little chin. "You know the drill, bottom up."

Scruff whimpered a little when he felt the thermometer. In a few seconds it beeped, and Helena looked at it. "Poor little guy has a fever."

Lauren loved this little dog so much. She was sorry for all the times that he aggravated her, especially when he had peed on her shoes and every other place that took his fancy. She just wanted him to wiggle his little tail and feel well again.

Lauren could have collapsed with relief as Gillian walked in, stood by her side and gave her hand a reassuring squeeze.

They both stood in silence as Helena took her stethoscope from around her neck and plugged it into her ears. She listened and moved it around Scruff's tiny little body. He looked so small. Helena took off her stethoscope and then started palpating around Scruff's body. When she got down to his stomach, Scruff winced and growled a little.

"Ahh, little tender there, aye buddy?" Helena said.

"What does that mean?" Lauren asked, suddenly

terrified, gripping Gillian's hand tightly.

"Honestly, Lauren. At this point, I think Scruff has a good old-fashioned stomach bug."

She let her body slump against Gillian's. "What? Dogs get those too?"

Helena nodded. "Oh sure. Most things we get, animals can get too. He's had all his injections, so I'm not worried about any of the big things. You know, these little guys especially, they're like little Hoovers. They suck up everything, and sooner or later they get sick from it. His heart is booming like a drum, so nothing scary there."

"Oh good," Lauren said tearfully. "He's just … Never been like this before. I didn't know what to think."

Unashamedly, Gillian wrapped her arm around Lauren's waist. She had never felt so secure and cared for in her entire life.

Helena patted her hand. "Oh, I know. It's scary and worrisome when our pets suddenly don't seem right. It's harder I think because they can't tell you what's wrong. If he could just say, 'My tummy hurts' it wouldn't be so scary."

Lauren nodded in agreement and sniffed as a tear rolled down her cheek.

"Let me go and get the medication. I'll be right back."

"Okay. Thank you."

She smiled and left. Lauren breathed a huge sigh of relief. "You're such a little stinker," she said rubbing his head. "Do you know what you put me through?" Scruff kept his head down but thumped his tail at her.

She turned to Gillian. "Thank you for being here for me."

"It's okay. You sounded like you were going to have a nervous breakdown on the phone. I can't have my little sex kitten all stressed out, can I?"

Lauren half laughed. Why did things have to be so complicated? She still hadn't made up her mind what to do about Calum. All she knew was that if she decided to go back to him she was going to be giving up her one true chance of happiness. But could she really live her life as a lesbian? What would she tell her mum and dad?

"Hey, what's got you looking so worried? I thought you'd be relieved now you know Scruff's going to be alright."

"I am," she said biting her bottom lip.

Gillian took her hand. "Lauren, if you've got something to say, I'm listening. If you've got regrets …"

"No! I don't. Never in a million years."

"So what is it? Have you made up with Calum? If that's what you're trying to tell me, it's no big deal really."

Lauren's heart sunk. "Is that it? Is that how little you think of me?"

Gillian shrugged her shoulders. "Lauren. I like you a lot. But I don't want to come between you and your husband."

"So what you're saying is that there wouldn't be a future for us if I were single?"

"I'm not saying that. What I am saying is that you've just slept with a woman for the first time in your life and are in the midst of all the heady sensations that come with trying something new. I'm not going to rush into anything where a month down the line you decide that it's not something you really want."

She swallowed her disappointment. "I wouldn't do that to you, Gillian."

"I know because I'm not going to let you."

Before Lauren could respond, Helena walked back in holding a paper bag. "I wouldn't be surprised if he has a little vomiting and diarrhoea for the rest of the day and tomorrow. He's acting like this because of the fever mostly, but the tablets should take his temperature down. Don't worry, he should be peeing on people's shoes again in no time."

Lauren's lips curved into a smile, but there was no feeling behind it. "That's good to hear." She tried to focus on what Helena was saying, but her thoughts were so much louder. Was she going to lose Gillian just when she'd found her? Was it really just an adrenaline rush for her? She didn't think so, but Gillian sounded so sure of herself when she'd said it.

Helena handed her the small package. "These meds don't taste good so hide them in something he really likes like a piece of meat or cheese."

When Lauren remained silent, Gillian spoke up,

"How long before he feels better?"

"Oh, I would say a day or two and you should see a marked difference. If you don't notice an improvement then bring him back."

Gillian nudged Lauren gently, shaking her out of her thoughts.

"Oh okay, thank you so much."

"No worries at all. Bye Scruff. I expect that tail to be wiggling next time I see you," she affectionately petted the little dachshund. "Take care now," she called out as they left the room.

As they walked down the corridor, Gillian pulled her aside. "Lauren, I've upset you haven't I?"

"No, you haven't. You were just being truthful. I've been walking around with my head in the clouds for too long. Not just about you but my whole life." She took a few steps forward.

Gillian hurried after her and grabbed her arm. "Lauren, this isn't about you."

She stopped suddenly and faced Gillian, her temper exploding at her meaningless words. "Jesus Christ, why does everyone always say that?" she said through gritted teeth. "It's not about you? If I'm the only one that's getting hurt, then who the fuck is it about then?"

Gillian backed up a hasty half step. "I just meant I'm not rejecting you, if that makes sense. I don't want you to do something that you're going to live to regret."

"Well, you don't have to worry, Gillian, because

I'm not going to," she said as she resumed walking and made her way to the desk to pay. Minutes later with Scruff wrapped up warmly in his blanket she stepped outside. Gillian was leaning against the wall waiting for her.

"My car is over there." She pointed in the direction of a black BMW convertible. "Can we go back to my place to talk?"

"No. I think I've done enough talking for the day." Lauren walked to the edge of the pavement and hailed a cab. It was time she stopped being a visitor in her own life and lived the way she wanted to live it. It seemed everyone around her was putting themselves first, and she needed to do the same. For the first time in her life, she heard her own voice. Not her parents. Not her teachers. Nor her friends. It was her own true authentic voice. It was as if she'd been released from prison, only the prison she'd been held captive in was her own mind.

Chapter Twenty-Nine

Every chunky wooden chair was taken in the small coffee shop situated on the corner of Old Compton Street. Gillian and Travis sat by the large, double windows that looked out onto the street.

"Seems like your day has been ten times worse than mine," Travis said as the waitress laid two coffees on the table in front of them.

Gillian toyed with the sugar bowl. "I feel like a Moaning Minnie complaining to you, especially at a time when you're going through all of this."

Travis patted her hand. "Gill, sweetheart, the world hasn't stopped spinning because I've got HIV. I don't have a monopoly on crap days. My issue is never going away – I've just got to deal with it. You, on the other hand …"

"Am a bloody fool." Why the hell had she reacted like that? Lauren had worn her heart on her sleeve, and she might as well have got a hammer and smashed it to pieces.

"That's one thing you're not," he said reassuringly.

"Oh yes, I am. I think I've really messed up this time."

He took a sip of his coffee and sank back against his chair. "What have you done now?"

"Nothing. I think it's more to do with what I didn't do. I think Lauren was trying to tell me she wanted something more than just a casual fling."

"And what's wrong with that?"

She lowered her eyes. "I don't trust her not to hurt me." There she'd said it. There wasn't any point in lying to herself any more. The feelings she had for Lauren scared her senseless.

Travis looked at her kindly, like a father advising her about her first breakup. "She's not Stella, Gillian. Jesus, I don't think there's any likelihood of you meeting another one like her in this lifetime."

She looked doubtful. "I know she's not unbalanced, at least I hope she's not. It's just that I don't want to go down that road where she turns around in six months and realises that being with a woman wasn't really for her," she said truthfully.

"Does she seem that fickle?"

Gillian shrugged her shoulders and looked around the café, before bringing her gaze back to Travis. "I don't know. I think she's been in a boring relationship for so long that now she's tasted some kind of freedom, she's like a child in a sweet shop. As we know there are only so many sweets you can eat before you get sick of them." She took a mouthful of coffee and replaced it on the saucer. "No, I think I've just got to resolve myself to the fact I'm going to be single for a little while longer."

Travis gave a little cough. "Well, you won't be alone on that score."

Gillian shot a look at him. "Why? What's happened?"

"Cody broke up with me," he said with a grimace. Gillian grabbed both his hands. "What? Why didn't you tell me? Here I am prattling on about my pathetic love life, and you're–"

"–It's no big deal. He couldn't cope with the guilt of having infected me."

"He bloody well should feel guilty." She was still outraged by his careless behaviour, but knew it was pointless going on about it. Like Travis had said, what was done was done.

Travis gave her a warning stare. "This is why I wasn't going to tell you. You've got to learn how to be more compassionate. Not everything is black and white in life, Gillian. There's a whole big grey area that we all tend to hide behind sometimes."

Gillian rolled her eyes as she retracted her hands and picked up her coffee again. "Okay, I apologise, grandfather of wisdom," she said bowing her head.

"Good," he said with a laugh.

"So what are you going to do?"

He raked his hand through his hair. "Carry on with my life. I still live in hope I'll meet my knight in shining armour."

Gillian smiled at him. "That's what I love about you, always the optimist."

"That's me," he said grinning.

Gillian's face softened, and she spoke with a tenderness that came straight from her heart. "Whoever you give your heart to will be the luckiest man alive."

Travis rolled his eyes. "Yeah, that's what I keep telling myself."

"It's true."

Travis waved his hand dismissively. "You'd think I'd know better at my age than to be blinded by love wouldn't you?"

"No, I wouldn't. It's called a human condition, and we're all afflicted by it regardless of how old we are."

He leaned forward in his seat and spoke in a low voice. "I know I was being naïve to think we could have moved on from this blip."

Gillian raised her eyebrows. "Blip?"

He gave her an impatient look. "But I think we both realised there would have always been trust issues along the line. I still had this small ray of hope that we could get through it. But …"

"Are you going to keep in touch with him?"

Travis nodded. "Yes. I've arranged for him to get some counselling at the centre. I'm glad he's agreed to it. He needs the support if what's happened to me is going to be avoided in the future. Talking of counselling, you, my dear, could use some yourself."

Gillian nearly choked on her coffee. "Me!"

"Yes, you. Don't you think it's time you faced your own demons?"

Gillian laughed wholeheartedly at such a ridiculous suggestion. "Demons?"

"Yes, it's not good to be so jaded at such a young age. You don't want to end up a bitter old dyke do you?"

Gillian winced at his choice of words. "It's not

me that needs therapy, it's the women I meet who seem to be the problem," she said firmly.

"Of course it is. What's that proverb from the bible? 'Why do you look at the speck of sawdust in your brother's eye and pay no attention to the plank in your own eye?' If you want to see the light at the end of the tunnel, Gillian, you have to open your eyes first."

Gillian slapped his hand playfully. "Knowing my luck they'll get covered with shit."

Travis burst out laughing. "I can't even blame your attitude on not having a shag in a while."

"No, you can't. Blame it on the fact that I can never seem to find a woman who doesn't come with a truckload of baggage."

Chapter Thirty

Lauren stared out of the cab window at the world passing by, each individual wrapped up in their own lives, experiencing their own little dramas. *What would one of those women do in my situation?* If she was totally honest, it was time for her to face the fact that her marriage was effectively dead. They had drifted too far apart to build a bridge. It had taken meeting Gillian for her to realise they didn't share the same interests, the same outlook on life or the same drive and motivation. They both wanted different things. How could life be made compatible with two almost incompatible people? *Do I still love him?* That is what this all boiled down to. *Yes, I do love him but I'm not in love with him and never have been.* The thought saddened her but if she was going to start making changes in her life she needed to be totally honest with herself. She knew what she wanted or rather who she wanted, and that was Gillian. But how was she going to convince her that she wasn't looking for a plaything to entertain her while she laboured in a dead marriage. Not in all the time she had been with Calum had she felt so alive. Never had his touch elicited such a reaction in her body. She had never been so consumed with a feeling of love? Was that right? Was it possible that she'd fallen in love with Gillian in such a short space of time?

Before she could think any further, the cab stopped outside her house. She paid the driver and held Scruff close against her chest as she walked up the path and into her house.

Oh crap, he's still here. She walked straight through to the kitchen and found Calum opening and shutting draws, totally oblivious to her presence.

"What are you looking for?"

He spun around in shock. "Lauren! I didn't hear you come in."

She looked down at the open drawer. "I asked you what you were looking for?"

"It's not important," he said closing it quickly.

"I thought you would have gone back to your mum's by now."

Lauren gave him the once over, trying to figure out what was going on behind those glazed eyes of his. She threw her keys on the table and lay Scruff in his basket near the radiator.

"Do you want a coffee?" he said walking over to the kettle.

"Is your phone broken?" She tried to keep the anger out of her voice.

"No, why?"

She let out a long sigh. "Why? Because, Calum, I've been phoning and texting you for the past couple of hours, to let you know I was taking Scruff to the vet."

He nodded his head as he leaned against the edge of the worktop. "Oh yeah, I got those messages."

"And?" She looked at him exasperated.

"And what?"

He seriously looked like he didn't have a clue. For the first time ever, she wondered how someone could be so brain smart but emotionally stupid?

She needed to buy time so she didn't scream at him. Opening the fridge door, she grabbed a bottle of water, twisted the lid off and drank deeply. When she was done, she turned back to him. Feeling a little calmer, she said, "You didn't think it was a good idea to reply or ask what was up?"

"I was busy. I figured if something were really wrong, you'd let me know what the vet said. So what's up with him?"

Calum walked over and petted Scruff, who looked at him with sorrowful eyes and thumped his tail.

"He has a stomach bug. He was acting really sick, and I was scared to death."

"Oh, well see? He's fine." He turned back to the kettle and took two mugs out of the cupboard.

Lauren clasped her hands in front of her, closed her eyes and took a deep breath. "Is that it?"

"Is what it, Lauren?" he said with irritation.

Lauren opened her eyes. "What's wrong with you Calum? You act like you don't even care about us?"

Calum stood up abruptly and smashed his fist on the worktop. His voice erupted with rage as his face turned crimson as he looked at her with pure hatred. "Where the hell is that coming from? Because I didn't text you about Scruff going to the fucking vet? Was it life threatening? Was he unconscious? Or was it you just blowing things out of proportion again?" he bellowed, making her wince. "What the hell did you want me to do? I'm not a vet. If he's sick, that's who needs to see him."

Lauren took a step toward him. She wasn't scared of him, and she wasn't about to let him think he could bully her into submission. Hadn't he been covertly doing that all these years? "You know what; I don't know who you are. I'm beginning to think I've never known you at all."

"Oh, I see," he said pounding his chest. "I'm the big bad wolf because I didn't come running and wailing because the dog's unwell. Do you know what Lauren? That's fucking life? People and animals get sick. End of."

Scruff jumped out of his basket and ran from the room. Lauren stood staring at Calum for a long while before speaking again. She was trying to figure out how they'd reached this stage in their lives. "Wow, what's wrong with you? I didn't know it was his stomach. All I knew was that he wouldn't move. And I contacted you for some support. But I should have known better shouldn't I. I've been so fucking blind."

"What's that supposed to mean?"

She squinted. "Exactly what it sounds like. I'm such a stupid idiot. This behaviour hasn't just come out of the blue. You've been like this ever since I've known you."

Calum gave a short abrupt laugh and walked over to the sink, keeping his back to her. "Lauren, you're being a little over dramatic don't you think? You're a grown up. I trust you to be able to handle things when I'm not available."

She walked up behind him and spun him around. "That's not the point, Calum. You're never available for me. I was scared and worried, and you couldn't take a minute to check on me."

Calum shook his head. "Well, you managed by yourself didn't you?"

"No thanks to you, if Gillian …"

Calum cocked his head. "Gillian? Gillian the accountant? How does she figure in this story?"

Lauren's eyes darted around the room. "Um … she called me to check if my mum wanted her to do anything else."

"Really? Why wouldn't she have called your mum directly?" The coolness had entered Calum's voice again, and Lauren couldn't care less.

"Because she called me, that's why. This is nothing to do with her. Why are you changing the subject?"

"I think it has everything to do with her, don't you think?" he snapped.

"What are you talking about?" There was something in his tone that made her wonder if he had something up his sleeve. It was now her turn to avoid eye contact.

"Oh, that's right revert to playing stupid. You're good at that."

"Calum, I wish you'd tell me what you're on

about."

"Likewise. You tell me," he said walking over to her. "Why, when a man is fucking his wife is she calling out a woman's name."

Stunned, Lauren stumbled back as if he had struck her. "What are you talking about?" Had she really done that? Called out Gillian's name. How could she have not realised?

"Oh cut the crap, Lauren. This gig is up. I know what you've been doing with her," he said staring down at her.

Her first impulse was to lie. She didn't know if she was strong enough to out herself to this man. If she did, she knew there'd be no going back. She pictured Gillian in her mind and thought about how strong she was, how in charge of her own life she seemed to be. She couldn't imagine her being afraid to show people who she really was. So neither would she be. "Yes, you're right and I'm sorry you found out this way, but I'm not sorry it happened with her."

"So, what? Are you a lesbian now?" Calum sneered.

Lauren stuffed her trembling hands in her jacket pocket. "Yes, I am," she said proudly.

They stared at each other, neither saying a word. As far as she was concerned there was nothing left to say. Their marriage was over. It had been from the beginning.

She walked past him and picked up Scruff's blanket.

"Where are you going?" Calum asked.

"I'm going to spend the night at my mum's, please be gone before I get back." She scooped up Scruff who sat in the hallway and headed out the door.

Chapter Thirty-One

Despite Lauren pushing the door with extra pressure, it still didn't open. She peered through the window and was surprised to see the showroom was empty. Even Lucy was missing from behind the counter. It was very unlikely her mother would have shut up shop early. *Something must be wrong.* She searched for her keys in her bag and quickly unlocked the door. As she stepped into the shop, she heard raised voices coming from the back office. Her initial thought was that there was a burglary taking place. Without thinking, she ran towards her mother's office, slowing down when she heard her dad's voice.

Oh my God, he's told her. Though she could hear her mother's tearful voice, she couldn't quite make out what she was saying. Lauren leaned against the wall. Should she let them know she was there or leave them to get on with it? Scruff's sharp bark took the decision out of her hands as her parents went silent and seconds later the office door opened.

"Oh, Hi, Mum," she said, placing Scruff on the floor.

"Oh, Lauren, this man's going to be the death of me." Jean puffed out her cheeks.

"What's wrong?"

Her expression betrayed nothing. "I shouldn't be dragging you into our mess. I'm sorry. Go home, Lauren."

Kens shoulders sagged. "She knows, Jean."

Thanks a lot dad! Now her mum was really going to hate her.

Jean exchanged a glance between them both. "Lauren knows!"

"Yes. But I only found out a little while ago," Lauren quickly protested as she saw her mother's eyes narrow into slits.

"I don't believe this," Jean said covering her face with her hands. "I just don't believe it."

"Jean, if only …"

Her hands fell from her face and she glared at him. "Just shut up, Ken. Just shut the fuck up!"

Lauren looked at her mother in astonishment. She had never heard her use the f-word in all of her twenty four years.

"Mum, I think you should listen to what Dad has to say."

Jean's facial expression changed from one of annoyance to horror. Her face paled and her mouth formed a hard line. "What can he say? Tell me! How can he explain wanting to wear women's clothes?" she shrieked.

Lauren rubbed her forehead. "I'm sure you can work though this–"

"–Ha! Maybe you should take your own advice and apply it to your own failing marriage," she said with a hint of sarcasm, before clamping her hand over her mouth. "Oh, I'm sorry, Lauren. I didn't mean it."

Lauren gave her a half-hearted smile. "It's okay. I

know you didn't. But don't you see, Mum, all of these secrets are tearing our family apart." She took a deep breath before continuing. "They're keeping us from being who we really are. Dad's not a bad person because he likes to dress up. You wouldn't think twice if I walked in here with a man's shirt on would you?"

"No, but–"

"–But nothing, Mum. It's just clothes. That's it. He isn't hurting anyone. Don't make him feel ashamed of being who he is. Maybe if our environment had been less judgmental this wouldn't be coming as such a shock to you. And my marriage wouldn't have failed because I wouldn't have married Calum in the first place. I would have followed my heart instead of trying to be what you wanted me to be."

"What are you talking about?"

"I'm in love …" Her voice wobbled slightly. She paused then cleared her throat. "With Gillian."

Jean stared at her open mouthed before saying, "Gillian? The accountant? Have you lost your senses?"

Lauren gave a wry smile. "No, Mum. I've found them and I'm not going to lie about who I am any more. If you can't accept that I'm still me and Dad's still the same man he was before you found out, you're going to lose us both."

Jean turned her attention to Ken, raw hatred in her eyes. "I will never accept you in any shape or form. You're a liar and a thief. You are dead to me now. Do you hear me? Dead!"

"Have it your way, Jean," he said hanging his

head as he turned and walked away.

"And what about me, Mum? Am I dead to you as well?" Lauren asked holding her breath.

Jean stared at her without saying a word.

Lauren knew this was the moment of truth. If her mother rejected her, there was nothing she could do. For the first time she felt free. She wasn't going back in her cage for anyone. "Mum, I've been hiding all my life. But I can't do it any more. I just can't."

Jean crossed her arms over her chest. "What am I supposed to say? That I agree with this ... this ... whatever it is."

"You don't have to agree, Mum." She broke off momentarily. "Just accept me for who I am."

"I can't, I just can't."

Emotion welled in her. There was no turning back. "Alright. I'll clear out my office and leave." She walked across the hall to her office and opened the door.

"Lauren."

She stopped abruptly and turned around. "It's okay, Mum. I know it's a lot for you to take in. Maybe I should have told you at a different time."

The frosty tension in the air thawed a little. "I don't know how this is going to work out, but please give me some time so I can get my head around all this." The expression on her mother's face softened.

Lauren cocked her head and nodded. "Fair enough."

With an open handed gesture Jean said, "You're

my life, Lauren and I don't want to lose you."

Lauren took a step towards her. "You don't have to if you don't want to. It's all down to you."

Suddenly to Lauren's astonishment her mother's body started to rack with sobs. "Oh, Lauren. I'm so sorry. I feel like I've failed you as a mother. If I would have been a better mother you wouldn't have to try and find a surrogate in someone else. "

Lauren choked up, and she quickly moved to her mother's side, encircling her in her arms. "Don't be silly. Believe me, I don't look at Gillian as a mother figure," she said soothingly.

"Are you sure?" Jean's voice was strained, as she looked up at Lauren with tearful eyes. "Then why now? You and Calum?"

Lauren patted her shoulder. "It was a mistake. It was a stupid bloody mistake."

"And I don't want to make the mistake of losing you." Jean straightened herself up and looked directly in Lauren's eyes. "I can't forgive or forget what your father has put me through, Lauren. But I will do anything and everything in my power to make things right between you and I, even if it means giving up my outdated prejudices," she said with a reassuring smile.

.

Chapter Thirty-Two

Lauren walked through her front door with a heavy heart. Her parents' marriage was over, as was her own. She'd come home as her mother had decided she needed some space to think things through. Lauren couldn't help but wonder whether telling the truth was well overrated – but what was the alternative? Living a life half lived?

Above she could hear movement on the landing. *Calum must be packing the rest of his stuff.* Taking two steps at a time, she side stepped the boxes at the top of the stairs.

"Oh, Lauren, shit. I thought you weren't coming back until tomorrow."

The sound of a glass smashing in the bathroom caught her attention. "Who's in the bathroom?" she said looking from Calum towards the bedroom door.

Calum's eyes widened and he dropped the box he was holding on the floor, then blocked the doorway. "Um look; I thought I'd have cleared out all my stuff before you got back."

"I said who's in there?" she said pushing past him.

"Look, Lauren," he said fast on her heels as she crossed the room to the en-suite and pushed the door open. Bending down on the floor was a sun-bleached blonde with a golden tan, gathering the broken glass.

"Who the hell are you?" Lauren barked.

The woman stood up and outstretched her hand. "Hi, you must be Lauren. I'm Isabella."

Lauren tilted her head to the side and stared at her wide-eyed. "Isabella. The boat?"

Isabella's features relaxed as she looked at Calum standing behind her. "Oh, so you know about me. Yes, I own the boat. I was going to say this was a bit awkward." She giggled nervously.

Lauren turned and glanced at Calum then back to Isabella. "If you don't mind, Isabella, I'd like you to leave my house."

"But–"

Lauren raised her hand. "–But nothing. Please leave. Wait in your car or the street, either one but please leave my house."

Calum held out his hand. "Come on, Izzy. Go and wait in the car."

Isabella put the broken glass in the sink. "Okay, look, I'm sorry about the glass. I'll pay for it–"

"–You're sorry about the glass but not about fucking my husband. Isn't that ironic?"

"That's nothing to do with me. Your problems are between you and Cal." She glanced at Calum as she passed him. "Can you be quick. My parents hate us being late."

They stood in silence until the front door slammed shut.

Lauren burst out laughing. "You're going to dinner with her parents."

"Come on, Lauren, don't be like that."

"Like what? In all the years we've been together, you hardly ever came to my parents for dinner. You hated it."

"I hated a lot of things to do with our lives."

"Then why didn't you ever say anything? It wasn't a bundle of laughs for me either." When he remained silent, she continued. "When did we become such good liars?"

He shrugged. "When we started living our lives the way other people wanted instead of trusting our own judgment."

"Do you love her?"

Calum cast his eyes to the ground and said nothing.

"Does she give you a reason for wanting to get up in the morning? Does the world feel like a different place because she's in it?"

"I dunno."

"Oh, Calum." She wrapped her arms around his neck. "Please don't settle for anything less again. It's not worth it," she said releasing him.

"Is that how you feel about Gillian?"

"Yes, it is and much more."

"Did you ever love me?"

She stopped for a moment and thought about his question. She thought about Scruff and her parents. About the antique shop and then about Gillian and the new life she hoped they were going to embark upon. In a flash, she knew what the answer was. "Not the way I love her, no."

The sound of the car horn caused them both to turn to the window.

"So this is it then?"

"Yep, this is it. Take care, Calum."

***

Lauren didn't really know where she was going until she realised she was standing outside Robin's. She peeped through the window and was relieved to see there were only a few people lurking about inside. *This is crazy but where else can I go?*

She stepped inside and slowly walked towards the bar. It was the same woman serving from the other night, and it looked like she remembered her.

"Are you becoming a regular?" Robin said coming to stand in front of her.

"Maybe. After the day I've had, I can see the attraction of spending all day in a bar."

Robin laughed. "It's on the house. What you having?"

Lauren smiled. "Oh, thank you. I'll have a brandy, please."

"Coming right up."

Within seconds, she'd handed her the drink, and Lauren knocked it back in one gulp. Digging into her pocket, she took out some notes. "Two more, please. And make them doubles."

Robin cocked one eyebrow. "Are you sure?"

Lauren nodded. The warm sensation spreading throughout her body was a sure sign she was on the right path.

"If you say so."

Robin poured two more drinks and moved away to serve another customer.

How could I have called out Gillian's name? At least it made sense as to why he'd reacted the way he had when she'd introduced him to Gillian that day. She slapped her head. That was the very night he'd come into the bathroom and made his "wanting freedom" speech. It was all coming together now. Should she just have confessed at the time about how she was feeling? She knocked back another brandy, moved the glass to the side and picked up the other one. She was starting to feel a little woozy now.

"Can things get any worse?" she said out loud, not expecting anyone to hear.

"I hope not," she heard a voice behind her say.

Lauren twisted round. "Gillian!"

Gillian grinned. "The one and only," she said as she slipped into the seat beside her.

"What are you doing here?"

"The same as you I think. Having a much-needed drink."

"Have some of mine," Lauren said nodding towards her glass.

Gillian picked it up and took a gulp, then handed it back to her. "How was the rest of your day?"

"Let's just say it's been bittersweet," Lauren said taking a sip of her drink.

"Do you want to tell me about it?"

Lauren burst out laughing and covered her face with her hands. "I can't. It's too embarrassing."

Gillian smiled. "Now I've got to know."

Lauren rested her head on the bar and let out a long groan. "Promise you won't laugh?"

"Cross my heart," she said making a sign across her chest.

She sat back up and turned to her. "Okay." She bit her bottom lip. "Calum told me I called out your name when we were, you know, doing the deed."

Gillian's cheeks coloured. "Oh! I don't know whether to be flattered or not."

"This was before we'd, you know, done it ourselves."

Gillian took several seconds to respond. "That was a bit of a conversation killer," she teased.

"And a relationship one as well, apparently." She dared to look into Gillian eyes. "So what happens next?" She was fed up of playing games; she needed to know where things stood between them, one way or another.

"Do you want to play a game?" Gillian asked.

Lauren was puzzled by her response but nodded anyway. "Sure."

"Truth or dare,"

Lauren laughed. "How old are we?"

"Come on. I'm serious, truth or dare?"

"Okay." She giggled. "Truth."

"Are you in love with a woman?" she asked.

Lauren locked eyes with her and the smile faded

from her face. "Yes."

"Do you want to be in a relationship with her?"

She nodded. "More than anything in the world." She leaned forward and kissed her gently before drawing back. "Now that's two. It's my turn."

Gillian nodded. "Fair enough."

"Truth or dare?"

"Truth."

"Do you love me?"

"Yes," Gillian said with a soft sigh.

Lauren's arms slipped around her back, bringing her closer. "Do you think you can trust me never to break your heart?"

"Most definitely."

Her grip tightened as she became more serious. "Gillian, I don't want anything to come between us. I need to know what happened with the married woman you were with. Did she leave her husband for you?"

Gillian's voice broke miserably. "In the end she had to."

"How come?"

Lauren watched as Gillian slowly pulled back her shirt. She frowned when she saw white faded scars littered across her chest.

A heaviness centred in the pit of her stomach. "Jesus, Gillian, what happened? Who did that to you?" she said, skating her fingertips across her skin.

Gillian spoke calmly. "The married woman I was in love with. She tried to kill me when I left the relationship."

"Oh my God, you don't think I–"

Gillian laughed. "–No, of course not."

Her eyes were filled with tears. "I would never hurt you, Gillian. Even if you were to reject me."

"Shhh," Gillian said placing her finger across her lips. "I'd never reject you, Lauren. I just don't want you to do something you're going to regret."

"Are you kidding me? The only thing I'd regret is not giving us a chance."

Before she knew what was happening, Gillian's lips were on hers. She closed her eyes and opened her mouth as Gillian's tongue crept forward; slowly, cautiously. She was instantly lost in the devouring hunger of her kiss.

Lauren framed Gillian's face in her hands and pulled back slightly. "I've waited a lifetime for you," she whispered to her. "You said at the beginning that our destinies were on a collision course."

Gillian's eyes narrowed. "And I meant it."

"But how could you have known?"

Gillian took her hands. "The very first time I looked into your eyes, my heart belonged to you."

"And mine to you." Lauren smiled. "So what does the future hold now?"

"Oh, we just do what any other normal couple does during the honeymoon period. We spend loads of time together having plenty of sex and eating–"

"–I have to tell you something. It might change the way you feel about me."

"Go on?"

"I can't cook."

Gillian let out a peal of laughter. "Oh no. That's something we're definitely going to have to fix."

"Okay, sorry carry on with the outline of our lives."

Gillian looked at her thoughtfully. "Where was I? Oh yeah, we'll travel and socialise. Wait until you meet my best friend Travis. You're going to love him. Speaking of friends, maybe we can get a companion for Scruff."

Lauren's pulse suddenly leapt with excitement. "It sounds perfect."

"And it will be most of the time, but Lauren, you need to understand something. If you decide to go down this route, at times it might not be easy."

"How so?"

There was a pensive shimmer in the shadow of her eyes. "It's a different world to the one you've been used to. Not everyone is as accepting as you might think."

She boldly met Gillian's gaze. "I'm sure of myself now and my rightful place in the world is with you." She kissed her, lingering and relishing every moment.

That is the most wonderful thing about life – you can never tell when that one moment will happen that changes your world forever. *Meeting Gillian on the train was the best moment of my life.*

Printed in Great Britain
by Amazon